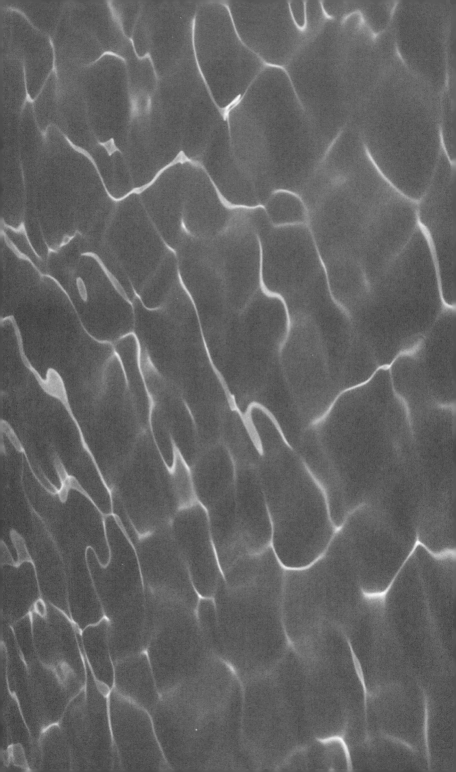

THE
ASTROLABE
OF THE SEA

SHAMS NADIR

Translated from the French by

C. Dickson

and with an Introduction by Léopold Sédar Senghor

CITY LIGHT BOOKS
SAN FRANCISCO

THE ASTROLABE OF THE SEA
Translation copyright © 1996 by C. Dickson
Translated from the French, *L'astrolabe de la mer,*
copyright © 1989 by Shams Nadir
First published in France by Editions Stock, 1975
All Rights Reserved
First published by City Lights Books in 1996
10 9 8 7 6 5 4 3 2 1

Cover design by Rex Ray
Typography by Harvest Graphics

Library of Congress Cataloging-in-Publication Data

Nadir, Chems.
    [Astrolabe de la mer. English]
    The astrolabe of the sea / Shams Nadir.
        p.   cm.
    ISBN 0-87286-314-X
    I. Title.
PQ3989.2.A96A913   1996
843 — dc20   96-2528

City Lights Books are available to bookstores through our
primary distributor: Subterranean Company. P.O. Box 160,
265 S. 5th St., Monroe, OR 97456. Phone: (541) 847-5274.
Toll-free orders: (800) 274-7826. Fax: (541) 847-6018. Our books
are also available through library jobbers and regional distributors.
For personal orders and catalogs, please write to City Lights
Books, 261 Columbus Avenue, San Francisco, CA 94133.

CITY LIGHTS BOOKS are edited by Lawrence Ferlinghetti
and Nancy J. Peters and published at the City Lights Bookstore,
261 Columbus Avenue, San Francisco, CA 94133.

CONTENTS

Introduction   vii

The Astrolabe of the Sea   1

The New Legend of the Winged-Storyteller   5

The Mountain of the Sacred Spider   21

The Cracks in Time   41

Reflections   61

Thar   69

The Two Calligraphers   81

The 366th Day of Leap Year   95

Back to Samarkand   111

INTRODUCTION
Léopold Sédar Senghor

The initiated—African men of letters—are well aware that Shams Nadir is the pseudonym of a well-known North African writer. His exemplary success stems first from the diversity of his talent. He is at once an essayist and a poet, but above all he is a man possessed of a dual culture, a vast culture, and he is as much master of his language in French as in Arabic. This is precisely what *The Astrolabe of the Sea* demonstrates. Make no mistake, the French text does more than translate the Arabic: it betrays the letter in order to preserve, as it renews, the spirit, by which I mean the style.

The very art of Shams Nadir the writer is at question and at stake in *The Astrolabe of the Sea*. Here then is a collection of original texts, Oriental in appearance— and it is not always clear where the tale leaves off and the poem begins—in which the ancient and the modern juxtaposed, far from being in conflict, coexist in symbiosis, clarifying and confirming one another.

Shams Nadir has brought up here once again the major problem. It is the problem of all writers who are not Euro-Americans (including the Japanese): and he has responded not with an essay—which he could have done—but with a literary work. The problem is knowing whether the writers of the Third World—I am using the term in its cultural sense—will continue to reproduce the ancient masterpieces, form and substance, structure and content, of their national literatures or if they will create new works, and richer ones, that are all the more human and more beautiful! Shams Nadir has resolved the problem in a magnificent way in the text of this book.

He has retained the Arabic substance: such themes as mad love, for example, and the actors, like the Winged-Storyteller, the Sacred Spider, the Calligrapher, the Black Man, and the Knight of Hearts. Not only the themes, but the style, the form, and above all that way of turning one's back on flat reality in order to deeply penetrate the real—to imagine the surreal as in *The Thousand and One Nights*. There is also the fact that, always true to the virtues of Arabness, Shams Nadir does not orchestrate the "dramatic impact" of the narrative, as is taught in the French lower schools. The plan, that is, the progression of his narrative, is not dramatic, but rhythmic, with breaks and repetitions, as in a poem, a song.

So, unlike certain writers of today, Shams Nadir has gone back to dip into the sources of Arabness. Like a plant drawing up essence to make its sap, he sank his roots deep down into his motherland. He did not convert to realism or other form of naturalism, nor did he commit himself to any sort of political engagement.

And yet there is a new man, a new Arab, in *The Astrolabe:* in the substance and in the form, the themes, and in the style. To be more accurate, there is a symbiosis of two cultures, and that is precisely what comprises all true revolutions.

Speaking of new themes, one finds here and there a criticism of Western civilization: of having rather than being, of standardization and bureaucracy instead of creation and poetry. In opposition to the West, a socialism with a human face is advocated, meaning democracy without distinction of race, religion, or sex. "In opposition" is a figure of speech, for in the narrative there is no geometric rigidity, but an allusive grace and something akin to smiling arabesques.

But now I've gone and touched upon the style. This style that intermixes all vocabularies, from the mysteriousness of pre-Islamic literature to the subtleness of Jean Giraudoux, a style that often gives way to the play of humor and fantasy with heartfelt emotion in order to teach us, to set us straight, enchanting us all the while. It is poetry in prose.

That is why Shams Nadir is today one of the best writers of Arabness. Even, especially, when he is writing in French. He is preparing, and announcing the Arab humanism of the twenty-first century.

THE ASTROLABE
OF THE SEA

Read in an ancient Persian manuscript, entitled
The Temple of Fire:

In a Muslim university in Shiraz, there was a copper astrolabe fashioned in such a way that he who once looked upon it, could not escape its fascination; for this reason the king ordered it to be thrown into the very depths of the sea so that men should not forget the weight of the concrete and the empire of the real.

The copper had oxidized since the immemorial immersion. Arms of coral tightly encircled the astrolabe, making it difficult to decipher. And yet, before his very eyes, the castaway Navigator saw unfolding, slowly, the fabric of dreams, immured far too long in the watery shroud.

In the woven creel, hauled back aboard the dhow with the aid of a great deal of stentorian huffing and puffing, there were, pell-mell, phosphorescent seaweed, carnivorous butterflies, golden sand, an amnesiac parrot, multicolored seashells, a handful of folk tales, some crystal flowers and more provisions, enough long-haired sea horses for reaching shore somewhere on the other side of the mirror.

Enough, in short, to wreak vengeance for the cruel order of the king of Shiraz who had condemned his people to see only the visible and, with the help of the sea foam's memory, attempt to decipher the tear in the veil.

"Listen, listen," said the Astrolabe, "I am going to tell you some tales . . ."

The New Legend of the Winged-Storyteller

*Show me the road that leads to the
land of the plant of life . . .*

*O Gilgamesh! There is no road. No
one has ever crossed the sea. Except for
Shamash, the sun, who could know how
to cross it?*

— The Epic of Gilgamesh

The arrival of the film's technical crew, although cut down to only eight persons, considerably disrupted life in the village. First of all, they had to be housed and fed. Not a single hotel, not a single restaurant had been built in the village or anywhere in the vicinity. Some of the inhabitants, more accommodating than others or more self-interested, agreed to provide them with bed and board in exchange for a modest compensation.

Then their incessant questions had to be graciously tolerated. Yes, graciously, for several reasons: these city folk, white as loaves of undercooked bread, mustn't go thinking that they had landed in the midst of unpolished boors or uncultivated primates (which is, alas, what the "tourists" who came from the city usually believed). Moreover, there existed a tradition

5

of hospitality and good manners in the countryside. Poverty should not erode these healthy principles upon which a well-earned reputation was built. Finally, everything that comes from the city being, in principle, suspicious, especially in these times of coercion and generalized spy-phobia, it was advisable to take precautions not to displease strangers who purported to be filmmakers and artists but who could well be agents dispatched by the authorities reporting to the Ministry of the Interior and of Public Security.

And yet this latest argument did not bear up against the frank smile of the head quizmaster, against the passionate interest with which the whole crew listened to their answers, and, in general, against the overall demeanor of these young men and women who had shown up in the village one spring day just as the wild poppies were reddening in the fields. The suspicion did not hold ground, especially in the face of the type of questions these young people were asking and the nature of the investigation they had begun. Indeed, conversation was essentially centered around the most popular folk tales among the village inhabitants!

After a period of reticence, the population grew more relaxed as the days went by. And everyone put in his little bit to defend and depict his favorite tale.

Shooting journal

It is said that six months of dreaming preceded the dictation of the Koranic text by the Angel. The allusion is clear: it shows that

Islamic thought acknowledges the multiplicity of reality in the successive stages of its ontological constitution and its phenomenological appearance.

For this reason I do not intend to make a flat-out documentary about a far-away village, with a presentation of the economic infrastructure and an analysis of the external attitudes and behavior of its inhabitants. I wish to go beyond this skin-deep and incomplete approach. I want to succeed in capturing another universe: a "double" of the world, invisible yet quite real, a world that is superimposed upon the concrete facts of our impaired perception.

The profusion of tales, narrated by the young and the old, surprised the members of the camera crew, even disoriented them, peopled their nights with strange and haunting images: an ogress giving birth through her big toe (improbable parthogenesis), a drowsy old black man named Luck, a majestic bird who bore the night along under the cloak of its wings.

Shooting journal

What's important for these people, is not so much the self-evident veracity of an accurate and banally didactic memory, but rather the exultation that a re-created story might bring to the present community. And little do verisimilitude or literal accuracy, judicious linearity, and causal deductions matter! Profusion of words, endless widening of meaning, backward twists, digressions, compartmentalized composition of the story, everything is aimed at fundamentally reconciling, within the same discourse, the waking and the dreaming state, the studied move and the spontaneous impulse, the coded and the unbounded, the concrete and the symbolic.

Little by little the stories were indexed, classified, labeled. The first concern was to calculate frequency. And it was a good thing. For, faced with the impossibility of shooting a film about each tale, it was necessary to choose only one as the starting point. And what could be a more democratic procedure than picking the tale that most frequently returned to the lips of the villagers?

An analysis of the records indicated the hands-down winner: the legend of the Winged-Storyteller (al-Taïr al-Bourni).

Shooting journal

> I would like to make a film with several voices, polyphonic, perhaps like a musical score.
>
> Several storytellers will succeed one another to give their own version of an episode of the tale. Perhaps they will even venture to embroider on the chosen theme to suggest other readings.

"Once upon a time there was a sultan who was pining away for lack of an heir. He had tried everything. His harem was overflowing with women who were each more desirable than the other and to whom he did not neglect to pay, each in her turn, his respects. But no womb germinated. None swelled. He had consulted the most knowledgeable doctors of his kingdom, drank the most bitter decoctions, swallowed the most heteroclite preparations, worn the most indecipherable talismans. Nothing worked. Until the day when a new ally, a powerful chieftain, gave him his daughter in marriage. The young woman conceived a child after the first month of their union. And the sultan's joy was great.

"Meantime, a war had broken out on the northern borders of the kingdom. The sultan departed at the head of his troops. He was absent for a very long time, and did not have the pleasure of being present at the birth of the child he had so desired.

"The situation in the palace was deteriorating. The jealous concubines were plotting openly. One night, a eunuch in the pay of spiteful rivals stole the infant, placed him in a basket, and abandoned him to the flowing waters of the river.

"A poor fisherman retrieved the makeshift cradle and, having no descendants of his own, adopted without further ado the innocent tenant of the frail bark, thanking providence, which fulfilled in this miracle his most secret desire.

"On returning home, he planted a fig tree for his adopted son. Feverish searches were undertaken in order to recover the royal infant. In vain. The sultan raged, rampaged, then for a long time lay prostrate with grief, which it seemed he would never overcome, all the more so since his attempts to fecundate once again the womb of the princess proved to be in vain. Time passed, and, in the sultan's enshadowed heart, winters followed one after the other.

"Time passed, and the young man grew strong in the splendor of his eighteen springs. His old father, despite difficulties, had secured for his adopted son—from whom he had carefully hidden the secret of his birth—an excellent education. And the young man was readying himself to join the respected brotherhood of imperial scribes.

"The fig tree had grown with the same vigor as the young man, who was in the habit of seeking out its shade in the hottest hours of the day. On the day of his eighteenth birthday, he had stretched himself out on the worn mat at the foot of his tree and was beginning to fall asleep when a strange shimmering light appeared on the quivering leaves of the fig tree. The tree spoke: 'The time has come for you to make a journey. You must find al-Taïr al-Bourni, the Winged-Storyteller. Only it can reveal to you the secret of your birth, for the fisherman is not your true father. . . .' A sudden force surged within him. He raised himself and, with no misgivings, without faltering, prepared for the journey."

From the shudder that ran across the chiseled features of a man who had recently returned from a long period of exile, I felt that something was going to happen, that we were going to depart from the familiar and conventional setting of the tale and that multiple variations were going to lead us to shoot some new legend of the Winged-Storyteller . . .

Sequence 2: The tale of the immigrant

"First of all, the young man went off in the direction of the setting sun. An invisible magnet seemed to be drawing him toward the West, beyond the pasturelands. He responded to the call since in any case no one could have indicated the exact place in which he might have had some chance of encountering the Winged-Storyteller and, consequently, the precise and suitable direction in which to guide his steps.

"For a long time he walked out beyond the borders. He crossed unknown countries, stayed in overpopulated cities.

"Truly, the lands of the Occident held astonishing discoveries in store for him. The perfectly straight streets, the amazing horseless carriages, the disquieting creature that snaked under the earth swallowing and spitting up clusters of busy men and women like a gigantic underground hive, the small boxes in which miniaturized people jerked about, the huge structures into which the multitudes piled, behind windows lit up in the night; all of this astonished him and filled him with admiration. And then he got in the habit of looking at the innumerable gazettes offered in the 'newspaper kiosks' (this is what the people of the faraway countries called these strange little houses). And he was amazed, once he was able to master their meaning, to see so many divergent opinions so freely expressed. This discovery increased his admiration tenfold.

"And he penetrated, endlessly, deeper into the lands of the West. But the more time passed, the more familiar he grew with this world. And then his admiration became measured: for he had discovered that the comfort which had been attained by this industrious civilization had its reverse side. It confined its beneficiaries in a kind of insidiously immobilizing cocoon. And he no longer looked upon the countless lights flickering at nightfall with the same eyes, for he now knew that each stood for still another solitude.

"And then he discovered something even worse: The fabulous animals that the peoples of the Occident had succeeded in domesticating, reducing them to merely docile executors (the 'machines,' as they were called), were not quite as passive as they seemed to be. On the contrary, their obedience seemed to him to be feigned. They served their masters but distilled subtle poisons for them all the while, and nature bore the wounds of the unsated appetite of men drunk with their conquests.

"He had the impression of being witness to a matricide that scandalized him. Moreover, he could not accept the rule that seemed to govern the collective behavior of this country: Man was valued not in his being but by his material worth, his possessions.

"Besides, upon close examination, this liberty that he had been so enthusiastic about in the beginning of his sojourn, wasn't it mostly specious? Now it was the absence of meaning that seemed to be the essential characteristic of this repetitive and, in many ways, comfortably impotent society. Yes, conformity to the norm had, perhaps, engulfed that magnificent libertarian impulse, turning it into a shapeless ferrous mass, perfunctorily discarded in some vacant lot, some machine cemetery of hopes under the placid moon.

"He started back down the road in the opposite direction, now convinced that it wasn't in these rich and powerful but putrefied regions that he was to find the Winged-Storyteller."

Shooting journal

> O, Scheherezade, forgive our iconoclastic liberty. You graced the king with three sons and a daughter who succeeded in bringing back the Winged-Storyteller, holder of the secret. Yours was the era of enchantment and pipes of splendor. Ours is that of knives and the piercing scream. But as we are reinventing this tale, your unforgettable image dances deep in our eyes. And the waves lap tenderly at your feet.

"The young man walked deep into the land toward the East. The same heavily urbanized landscapes unfolded before his eyes. But the customs of the inhabitants of these countries seemed different to him. Here too, the fabulous mechanical animals had been domesticated. But it seemed to him, on first sight, that the advantages that they dispensed were more equitably distributed. He was thrilled to see that education extended even down to the most underprivileged and that medical care was free. He had, therefore, good reason to believe that it would be in these lands of justice that he would have the greatest chance of discovering the Winged-Storyteller whose song was truth.

"But his searching proved to be in vain. The more time that passed, the more his initial enthusiasm became measured. He had in vain sought out those gazettes with so courageously divergent opinions, the reading of which had been his principle pleasure during his stay in the lands of the West. In these countries only one opinion could be legitimate, and whoever diverged from it was sent away to disturbing places where care was taken to rectify his judgment and, with the aid of the appropriate treatment, to extirpate from his mind any 'antisocial tendencies.' One day he discovered in a vacant lot a gigantic gilded cage. Its bars were snipped and twisted in places. He realized that the Winged-Storyteller, momentarily tempted by the promises of these lands, had deserted them when the garrote of the bureaucrats strangled the prophetic song of the founders. So, he continued on his way and, guided by the evening star, he went off in the direction of the Boreal lands."

Shooting journal

The myth of Sisyphus now comes to my mind. It wasn't at all his not being able to push that ridiculous boulder up to the top of the mountain; in fact, it was his not being able to reconcile, for his progeny—ourselves—justice and liberty!

Sequence 4: The tale of the mystic

"Our hero landed on snowy shores. Here, everything seemed to have been conceived for man's happiness. Yet, great was his astonishment to find that, despite all the happy premises, happiness seemed to be lacking. Was it due to this unfortunate obsession of *overfill* that he had encountered all along his peregrinations through these countries so richly endowed by the gods? No land could be left in peaceful fallow, no place was deserted, no time filled simply with promises. For every place and for every thing, the infinite voracious industriousness of the inhabitants of these countries invented chores to be done, spaces to be domesticated, lands to be sown, receptacles for garnering. This willpower and this force were admirable. And yet, he could not completely admire them, for both seemed to be endeavors to fill the breaches, the fissures in being. No, without a doubt, life, for him, real life, was elsewhere. Unless his diagnosis was false from beginning to end, and the inconsiderately high suicide rate in these Boreal lands to which nature had so generously given unlimited resources should be solely imputed to the infinite languor of the nights, or else to the desperate succession of shadeless days, lasting half the year . . . If the Winged-Storyteller had alighted on these shores, it imagined, at the time, that here could well be its last stop. Long nights or orphaned days, the magic winged creature might perfectly well have succumbed to the fate of those who allow themselves to be numbed by the fatal languor of the Aurora Borealis. So, he shook himself to his senses and set out for the South."

Relations between the camera crew and the villagers had evolved. The mutual distrust characteristic of their initial contacts had given way to a somewhat affected but quite real cordiality. Now, from time to time, the villagers invited the crew to share meals with them. Some went even so far as to exchange bits of conversation upon subjects that were less and less innocuous. And yet, despite the courtesy of their hosts, the filmmaker-sociologists felt that the exchanges fell far short of hitting home and that whole reaches of their hosts' mode of thinking remained obscure and off-limits to them.

We had come with outstretched arms, wearing our hearts on our sleeves; and our arms had enfolded only emptiness, our hearts had only beat to the rhythm of absence.

We will be all ears for the people, we had pompously said, we will awaken the creative latencies of the popular masses, we had immodestly declared. We had wished to place Prince Charming's kiss upon the ice-cold lips of Sleeping Beauty, that she should softly shake herself from her dreams. And now here we are, weary sentinels, trackers who have lost their way, faced with the ashes of our own incertitude.

Sequence 5: The tale of the bearded man

"He set out for the South and hope spurred him on. Was it not from these so long enslaved countries that rose in the night the fiery words that would light the struggle of the outcast and the humiliated?

"One day, in the lands of the ancient Ramayana and the Wayang, led by the legendary Arjuna, sprung from the nether-regions, the states-general of all liberated peoples met and a great rainbow stretched from the Balinese shores to the Andean foothills. On that day the Winged-Storyteller spread the immense airship of its wings and took to song. At the other end of the liberated lands the Plumed Serpent answered it, from beyond the brazen sierra. The Gods danced in the savannahs and

17

the tropical forests. And then, for a moment, there was the exhiliaration of the rolling waves.

"Yes, he thought of all this and hope spurred him on.

"But soon his pace slowed and his steps began to falter. For that which he could now see of these countries, once boiling over with dissent and with hope, threw him into a great quandary. Over these parched lands, poverty trailed its usual shabby rags, and injustice, the eager beast of prey, sank its fangs into the same astonished flesh.

"The sound of boots had drowned out the crackling of the flames, and in the marble palaces the local potentates had replaced the old foreign master."

"When he reached the blessed regions where the earth's entrails had given birth to the liquid black gold, he believed for a moment in a miracle.

"The wealth would, without question, aid the former outcasts in finding the solution that would enable them to tame the Winged-Storyteller.

"But a visit to the marketplaces of the first towns he encountered along the road persuaded him that his hopes had been futile.

"The Winged-Storyteller was there, to be sure, only in several thousand lifeless effigies. Its emblazoned image, fashioned out of various precious metals, adorned the imported articles that heaped up in the shops: televisions, tape-players, perfumes, automobiles, refrigerators.

"At times, in some public squares, he even happened to witness sumptuous popular celebrations in which enormous straw-stuffed forms representing the Winged-Storyteller would be offered up to the fervent crowds that were gathered.

"He saw huge stuffed Winged-Storytellers set on marble pedestals, besieged by swarms of people.

"It was when he realized that all the totems were turning their backs to the sun, that he resolved to turn back and go home."

Sequence 6: End related by the collective of village storytellers

"He resolved to turn back and go home. He prepared himself to accept misery and hunger and archaism and myth, not as immutable destiny but as the actual contours of his life. Yes he would take the road back to his ignorant brothers, back to those wastelands. And no haunting obsession—not even that of his origins and his identity—could separate him from his own kind. Wisdom was, in the end, being reconciled with one's self. He hadn't the slightest doubt that if the Winged-Storyteller had existed and if he had been able to lay his hands on it, it wouldn't have told him anything different.

"He returned to the house of his old father, the fisherman, whom he hugged close to his breast for a long time. He went out into the middle of the courtyard and, with the aid of a pick, uprooted that tempter, the fig tree. Its branches would serve to warm the long winter nights that were approaching, when he would need to be seriously preparing for his examination for admission into the elite corps of the palace scribes . . ."

"The revolution broke out and the head scribe instituted the First Republic.

"An old eunuch smiled at destiny's obstinacy: The child abandoned by him to the flowing waters of the river had reappeared to succeed his royal father who, till the end, had not known him! It was of little importance to the old sceptic that the throne be called by one name or by another. Providence sealed, in his eyes, the links of an endless chain . . ."

Shooting journal

The last scene is in the can. Tomorrow, we will be leaving the village. What will become of its inhabitants after the effusions and effervescence of these days of shooting? Will we carry away with us, petrified deep in our reels, the incredible kaleidoscope of dreams? Will we suck out, like bloodless vampires, the last drop of dream?

At daybreak, the crew got back into the rickety bus that was to carry it home. The motor started up after a few reluctant hiccups and the vehicle lumbered off in a cloud of dust. For a long time, in the wake of its passing, grains of sand hung motionless in the disturbed air and shone iridescent in the early morning light.

Little by little, the dust thinned and the trail regained its everyday aspect.

The Mountain of the Sacred Spider

The morning sunlight danced upon the bronze sword, where now not a trace of blood remained: "Would you believe it, Ariadne," said Theseus, "the Minotaur scarcely defended himself."

— J. L. Borgès. The Home of Asterion

Preparations for the ceremony were drawing to an end. The starry night resounded with the pounding of hammers and with orders called out by weary overseers. In the central square of the city, workers were busying themselves after having drunk their mint tea, provider of new strength and appeaser from time immemorial of the grumblings of half-empty stomachs.

The totem representing the tutelary god spread its shadow over the needy ants bustling about at its feet.

Tomorrow the sun would shine gloriously on the menacing statue and the government would specify to the assembled people the offerings that would need to be made in order to humor the exacting god.

At the cock's first cry, a veiled multitude of women emerged from the *ghorfas,* troglodyte dwellings carved into the hillside, and their silhouettes stood out darkly against the vague light of dawn. They were going to prepare *raghifs,* the bread that it was customary to eat on this holiday morning.

Kadath awakened foggily to the familiar clinking of kitchen utensils. He imagined his old mother busying herself with the preparation of his breakfast. How proud she was of him! How satisfyingly his success in the governor's armies had atoned for the tragic days that had followed his father's death! And the way that she would look at him every time he came home fully harnessed in the magnificent uniform of a senior officer for the governor's armed forces. He thought with delight in his half-sleep of another woman who was soon to share his life: his fiancée Kédar, who was so beautiful that the water in the stream grew cloudy when she passed. Was it the mirror of the water that was perturbed by having to reflect so much perfection, or the lovesick blushing of a water jinn? His old mother was calling him. His breakfast was waiting. He jumped out of bed and began to wash. He must be perfectly presentable for such a memorable day.

The enigmatic and vaguely cynical heads of dromedaries stuck out above the impatient crowd. Excited children chased one another through adult legs. The sun flashed its incandescent mask over the square crucified by the shadow of the totem. The people were awaiting their governor's speech. Suddenly, at one end of the square there was a commotion. The governor's escort was clearing the way for His Excellency by pushing the crowd back from around the official tribune. The governor and his Council appeared to the cheers and acclamations of the crowd. Kadath felt more than slightly proud at being present as a senior officer of the armed forces, along with the dignitaries in the governor's entourage. From down in the swarm of the crowd two pairs of eyes must be affectionately watching his every move. His old mother was doing her best not to miss his slightest gesture, while his beautiful armor must be be dazzling the most bewitching eyes in the whole region with its bright gleam.

The governor waited for silence to be restored and then spoke:

> My dear people, my dear children:
>
> As every year, at this same time, I have called you together in order to inform you of the desires of our dearly beloved God: the Sacred Spider.

The audience was becoming more and more impatient but the governor seemed to pay little heed. He related, in minute detail, his embassy. And to begin with, the ritual of offerings and of purification, thanks to which he had prepared himself to encounter the Face of the God.

He spared them no detail: the three nights of prayer and fasting in the mausoleum; the psalmodic procession he had led out to the Turtles' Oued; the offerings that he had deposited there; the return to the mausoleum, the ritual sacrifice of a black ram, a red rooster, and a white heifer at the foot of the ancient mulberry tree; the details of his lonely expedition through the labyrinth of valleys to the secret center of the Sacred Mountain; finally the miraculous meeting with the tutelary god.

"Our beloved God demands, as he does every year, half the harvest and a young virgin. His choice this year has gone to Kédar, the daughter of our esteemed chamberlain."

In the silence that followed the proclamation, a cry rang out. A milling movement ran through part of the audience. Compassionate arms lifted the body of the inanimate maiden. Silence closed back in.

Suddenly, a young officer up on the tribune stepped forward and, in a firm voice, called out the ritual formula: "I protest and I challenge."

The silence persisted. The governor turned in disbelief toward his companions and stared at the officer. He hesitated before responding, then acquiesced with a short nod of the head and, without a word, stalked away, with a great angry sweep of his cape. His attendants, momentarily disconcerted, hurried to follow him and Kadath, the imprecator, found himself alone on the official tribune. The public gathering had been irremediably interrupted. But what could have been done to avoid this? In all living memory, the laws of the city had always authorized anyone to challenge the divinity if they wished. It is true that the rare mad fools who ventured the undertaking, never returned from meeting the wrathful God face to face.

The sky strung itself with stars for the lovers' last night, and the heartbreak of their farewell in no way weakened Kadath's resolve. Rather the contrary. And it was with a heavy heart but a lively and resolute step that he left Kédar to begin preparations for his expedition. His mother dared not say a word to him but sat up all night in a corner of the room where he had lain down. Her eyes shone in the dimness and the slightest ray of light glimmered in her silent tears.

At dawn, he mounted his steed and, at a full gallop, headed out toward the still shapeless mass of the sacred mountains.

It was the very soft whistling of the arrow, cutting through the air toward him, that prompted him to drop from his horse instinctively. The sharp point glanced off his left shoulder and, continuing its slowing course, drove itself into the crest of a nearby dune. He remained crouching down in the sand for a moment. Yes, it was true, he had indeed just survived an attempt on his life before even reaching the foothills of the Sacred Mountain. Perhaps it was the work of some sentinel posted out here, on orders from the wary God, and who was thus carrying out his duty as watchman? He heard, all of a sudden, the sound of horses running off.

Cautiously, he rose to find to his amazement two horse-men hurriedly disappearing, in a cloud of sand that prevented their being identified, in the direction of the city! This did not fail to provoke a certain uneasiness in Kadath. If this attempt were not the deed of some sentinel in the service of the Sacred Spider, who in the city could gain by killing him and preventing him from carrying out his challenge? But the youthful ardor of heros is never long abated by questions of this sort. And Kadath chased them from his mind in the very movement of dusting himself off and straightening his clothing. Then, retrieving his mount, he began walking once again toward Last Sleep Gorge.

All day long, keeping pace with his horse, Kadath walked farther into the deep valleys. From time to time he would call out to the Spider and renew the terms of his challenge. But the lonely echo of his voice fading slowly away was his sole response.

A host of bats carried in, on its wings, the veils of night. So Kadath brought his horse to a halt, had a frugal meal; then having discovered a propitious rock escarpment, rolled up in his blankets and went to sleep.

At first it had been the sounds coming up from the ravine that had pulled him from his sleep. He listened closely. They were guttural sounds chanted in a very soft, almost plaintive tone. Silently he pulled himself up to the edge of the promontory. The moon had slipped behind the clouds and a dark shadowy pit deepened beneath him. The ball of fire dancing at his feet stood out brightly against the darkness. He suppressed a shudder of fear and anxiety at the thought that the Spider could have surprised him in his sleep if it hadn't been for this odd idea of chanting these words that he could not understand.

"Ibo loco. Legba atibo . . ."

At the touch of his sword handle he regained confidence and, after raising himself halfway, he rushed suddenly down the slope, brandishing his arm.

The moon reappeared between the clouds and what he saw as he was running, brought him up short.

A bald giant, his head coated with phosphorus (so that's what the ball of fire had been), ceased his dancing around a half-filled barrel of water and looked at him, it seemed to Kadath, in both fear and gratitude at the same time. A moment went by. Then the giant knelt on one knee and bowed down at his feet.

"Loa, intercessor, o captivating God. May thanks and praise be upon you. You have made it possible for your humble servant to capture the moon, Queen of the night and of maleficence, in the water of the barrel." The Bald Man, his body seized with twitching, seemed unable to keep himself from raving on.

Kadath realized that the possessed man credited him for his "victory." Puerile combat—how could one fear the moon and make of her a common caster of spells—and a laughable victory. The poor fool wouldn't recover from his hallucinations anytime soon! Kadath shrugged his shoulders, cursed inwardly at this troublesome person, and scaling up the pile of rocks without even a glance in the direction of the Bald Man, who was still bowing behind him, wrapped himself back up in his blanket and went back to sleep with difficulty.

The bemused moon said not a word, but thought nevertheless:

"To each his illusions and his myths. Those that I weave have at least the advantage of being made from threads of silver light."

The next day, Kadath began walking again.

For six days, he walked.
For six days, he called to the Spider.
For six days, he reiterated his challenge.

But nothing, only the echo of his voice fading slowly away, responded to his calls, his challenges, his quest, which grew more anxious from hour to hour.

On the seventh day, his despair had grown beyond all limits, for now the impressive height of the Bronze Gate, which marked the end of the Gorge, was looming into view. He had reached the final step of his journey.

This didn't prevent him from continuing to call out with all his might to the Spider and to furiously renew his summons to single combat.

But night fell and the Bronze Gate drew nearer without the smallest creature deigning to respond to his appeal.

He sank into despair.

He brought his horse to a halt and was about to jump down from his weary mount. But he checked himself, for just then, from behind a small hill of sand crowned with bristling cactuses, he saw the fitful glimmer of a campfire. A wan light, to be sure, yet a very real one that indisputably indicated a presence.

Suddenly, along with a resurgence of hope, he recovered his failing strength and, taking infinite precautions, he began crawling up the sand hill after having left his horse a little farther off. When he reached the crest, he could clearly distinguish the fire and, sitting with its back turned, a figure cloaked in what seemed to be an old burnoose.

At first he was surprised that the Spider—for it could only be She out in the immensity of this solitude where, for seven long days, aside from the mad Bald Man seen briefly on the first night, he had not encountered a living soul—could have this frail, almost feeble appearance. Then he found that it keenly satisfied him: the duel promised to be less formidable than he had expected. He put his hand to the hilt of his sword and walked resolutely toward the figure with its back turned.

At the sound of his steps, the figure swung around. And Kadath clearly distinguished the chiseled features and majestic white beard of an old man with a peaceful and slightly frightened look on his face. The man spoke. "Why this threatening and fierce bearing, young stranger? If your intentions are spurred by greed or by malevolence, you should best be on your way. I am an old solitary hermit whose death could in no way profit you."

Stupefied, Kadath strove to muster an engaging smile. Then he began to recount his adventures to the old man in order reassure him of his intentions.

The hermit listened in silence to the young man's tale. From time to time, a pained smile would flash across his face.

At the end, the old man let out a sad laugh and said, "My dear child, in the forty years since I retired to this desolate place, I have had quite enough time to explore all of these lands, to get to know their remotest recesses. And I can guarantee you that with the exception of a few animals, the mad Bald Man whom you met on the first night, and myself, no living creature dwells in these parts. No spider-faced god has ever honored these stones with its presence.

"The Spider is a dream, a figment of the ailing imagination of your fellow citizens, the expression of their alienation and the instrument of their enslavement."

At first, Kadath could not bring himself to believe it. Then, little by little, he gave in to the old man's arguments and acknowledged the simple truth. Just as the Bald Man entangled in the moon threads of his own fantasies, he and his fellow citizens had lived imprisoned in an enormous spiderweb that their resignation on the one hand, and the use that the authorities had made of it on the other, had woven to dull their consciousness.

Joy overwhelmed him. He hurriedly took leave of the old hermit, not without first having thanked him for opening his eyes, and rode back at a gallop the way he had come to carry the good news to his fellow citizens.

He rode for six days and soon the other end of the Gorge came into view, hastening his pace considerably.

A cloud of sand formed ahead of him; it was coming out to meet him. He could soon make out three riders. He was familiar with their silhouettes. He recognized the full black cape of the governor billowing out as his horse galloped along and, on either side, two of his close advisers.

The place where they met was just under the promontory where he had taken shelter for his first night's sleep.

The governor had a sly smile on his face. He observed Kadath in silence for a moment, then said, "So? Our hero has returned. Now he knows the secret of our power. He's very proud of himself. Well, young fool, you won't be for long. Because that secret will keep you company in your grave." As he spoke, one of his companions had calmly begun to arm his bow, and was preparing to shoot in the direction of Kadath, who at such close range realized that the hour of his death had come.

Three whistling sounds rang out, and almost simultaneously the three riders clasped their hands to their chests where three daggers had just found their mark.

Without reacting, Kadath watched as the three bodies crumpled and then slowly slipped down over the sides of their mounts. Then he looked up in the direction of the voice that was speaking to him:

"Loa, intercessor, o captivating God. Permit your humble servant to come to your rescue." He then realized that to repay his own debt the Bald Man had just saved his life. He gave a smile of thanks and a friendly wave of the hand and continued along his way.

Intrigued by the impromptu departure of the governor, the populace had gathered near the entrance to the Gorge to await the critical events that, they hadn't the slightest doubt, were sure to occur. They even delegated the most courageous or the most curious in their ranks to act as lookouts. These select few cautiously ventured into the first foothills of the Sacred Mountain.

A long time passed and the frenzy of the first gathering was beginning to wear thin when one of the lookouts reappeared. He was extremely excited and called out in a broken voice, "Kadath is coming back . . . the savior is near!"

Kadath did not have time to complete his homeward journey before clusters of people were circling around his horse, buzzing with unleashed joy and anxiety. When he came out onto the square marking the limits to the city, the sound of the acclamations swelled to a roaring surge: "Long live the saviour. Long live the hero. Long live the miracle man, Kadath, the city is at your feet. . . ." For a time, he made a brave attempt to rise above the huge clamor in order to deliver his message and give an exact account of his incredible adventures. But what was his voice compared with the noise of this tide of exultation? Besides, he told himself, how could he have the effrontery to dampen the joy of his fellow citizens on this memorable day of national liberation? It would be wiser to leave to tomorrow the issuing of his message. Yes, tomorrow, he would tell them the truth.

And the celebration went on. Carried on the shoulders of the crowd, Kadath was taken to the governor's palace, now empty of its principal tenant, but who, in the general atmosphere of euphoria was concerned with that?

He scarcely had time to catch sight of his fiancée and note the absence of his old mother. He was later to learn that she had died of sorrow, and he was truly bereaved.

At the palace, preparations were made to celebrate the new occupant of the premises. Kadath was taken in hand by gracious servant women who bathed, massaged, and dressed him in embroidered silk and brocade. Afterwards, the chamberlain showed him the royal apartments, then the gynaeceum where he had time to take note of the beauty and variety of race of his concubines. The chamberlain, very obliging, left him so that he might take a legitimate and very necessary rest after his heroic escapade and before the official reception, which was to close this historic day.

He refreshed himself with savory delicacies and admired his concubines, attentive to his slightest desires, but did not feel free to make use of one of them to satisfy an irrepressible sexual desire. He thought that Kédar should be the first to receive his effusions, though perhaps, later on. Well, he would see. . . .

He summoned his chamberlain once again and issued orders for his marriage to be celebrated that very night.

The ceremonies celebrating his triumphant return and his marriage were unforgettable. The fervor of the people overflowed in a floodtide of dancing and singing. The celebrations were marked with a display of magnificence never seen before.

The city celebrated very appropriately the return of the prodigal son, the heroic saviour.

But the next day, he had difficulty in waking up. The fine dishes, the abounding wines and the voluptuous pleasures he had freely indulged in throughout that memorable night had made his eyelids heavy and deadened his conscience. And already, the chief of protocol was there urging him to assume his new responsibilities. This first day was to be consecrated to the *Baïa,* a traditional Muslim ceremony of allegiance, and the representatives of the most important institutions —the Syndicate of Merchants, the League of Bureaucrats, the Association of Middlemen, the Union of

Property Owners, and the rest— were already gathered in the throne room to pay their allegiance to the new governor, Hero of the People, Saviour of the Nation. (He learned that, hereafter, this was to be his official title and whoever did not conform, by forgetting to mention part or all of the complete title, would be liable to appropriate punishment; he admired the diligence and know-how of his services.)

While his servants were preparing him, he had time to remark to himself that a governor's schedule was definitely very full and that today, he would certainly not have time to tell his people about his adventurous journeys and his incredible discovery but that, without a doubt, tomorrow, or the day after or some day soon, he would be able to call a public meeting in which he would make these revelations. Dressed at last, he motioned to the chief of protocol and started out toward the throne room to assume his new responsibilities.

Time passed. First there were the official holidays: the seventh day of his return, the second week, the first month, the three-month commemorative service, and so on. On each of these occasions, the inhabitants of the city, duly "encouraged," donned their holiday finery once again and the wine flowed freely. And then there were the happy personal events: his first child, his second marriage, his own birthdays. And on each of these occasions the properly "motivated" city shared in the joys of its dearly-beloved governor, Hero of the People, Saviour of the Nation.

But, you see, the celebrations could not resolve any of the economic problems confronting the country, and for some time, the secretary to the Treasury had been complaining. Finally one day, what everyone in the governing body feared most happened: The coffers were found completely empty.

A restricted Council meeting of Ministers was immediately convened and the appropriate means and ways of keeping the Treasury afloat were discussed.

They shouldn't expect a surplus of productivity: The population had not adapted to the newly imported techniques.

Technical assistance? Not a single perspective on that front. Aside from the fact that most of the land and the means of production had already been sold to the highest bidder, the insolvency of their new credit had become more than hypothetical. And the powerful Empire of the West was quite willing to continue to support the regime militarily and politically, but, more and more often, turned a deaf ear concerning the question of reinflating the leaky coffers. So . . .

After an in-depth examination, the Council arrived at the following conclusion: to levy new taxes. Even though he admitted that it was the sole solution, the governor was troubled, "What will the people think of such a measure? How could they accept, coming from their hero and their saviour, these excessive amounts?"

Oh naturally, Kadath didn't have to worry himself about the violent reactions that such a measure might provoke: His police force was first-rate and his army well-trained by the advisers that the friendly powers put at his disposal. But after all, he had his image to worry about and did not resign himself willingly to seeing it tarnished.

It was just then that his minister of Propaganda spoke up. Kadath had always admired this elegant and crafty man. He had even thought of making him his vizier, but a hidden instinct had always stopped him: too crafty; one never knows, he might be tempted to unseat him. "Sire," said the subtle adviser, "suffer me to think that there exists a solution to this problem. It would consist in spreading the news of the resurrection of the Spider. Oh, naturally, during your glorious combat, you had crushed, mortally wounded Her. But just as the Phoenix is reborn from its ashes, She has now healed her wounds and come back to life, with ever more exacting demands. Of course, the Cabinet, under your enlightened guidance, is already setting about researching the appropriate strategy to rid us of this divine calamity once and for all, but in the meantime, what can we do, except acquiesce to Her demands? The people will pay the divine tithe while placing all its hopes in your capacity to solve, sooner or later, the problem once again."

The proposition was adopted without further discussion and the means of application were determined immediately.

Preparations for the ceremony were drawing to an end. The starry night resounded with the pounding of hammers and with orders called out by weary overseers. In the central square of the city, workers were busying themselves after having drunk their mint tea, provider of new strength and appeaser from time immemorial of the grumblings of half-empty stomachs.

The totem representing the tutelary god spread its shadow over the needy ants bustling about at its feet.

Tomorrow the sun would shine gloriously on the menacing statue and the government would specify to the assembled people the offerings that would need to be made in order to humor the exacting god.

At the cock's first cry, a veiled multitude of women emerged from the *ghorfas,* troglodyte dwellings carved into the hillside, and their silhouettes stood out darkly against the vague light of dawn. They were going to prepare *raghifs,* the bread that it was customary to eat on this holiday morning.

Hiram awakened foggily to the familiar clinking of kitchen utensils. He imagined his old mother busying herself with the preparation of his breakfast. How proud she was of him! How satisfyingly his success in the governor's armies had atoned for the tragic days that had followed his father's death! And the way that she would look at him every time he came home fully harnessed in the magnificent uniform of a senior officer for the governor's armed forces. He thought with delight in his half-sleep of another woman who was soon to share his life: his fiancée Rabiaa, who was so beautiful that the water in the stream grew cloudy when she passed. Was it the mirror of the water that was perturbed by having to reflect so much perfection, or the lovesick blushing of a water jinn? His old mother was calling him. His breakfast was waiting. He jumped out of bed and began to wash. He must be perfectly presentable for such a memorable day.

The enigmatic and vaguely cynical heads of dromedaries stuck out above the impatient crowd. Excited children chased one another through adult legs. The sun flashed its incandescent mask over the square crucified by the shadow of the totem. The people were awaiting their governor's speech. Suddenly, at one end of the square, there was a commotion. The governor's escort was clearing the way for His Excellency by pushing the crowd back from around the official tribune. The governor and his Council appeared to the cheers and acclamations of the crowd. Kadath felt more than slightly proud at being present as a senior officer of the armed forces, along with the dignitaries in the governor's entourage. From down in the swarm of the crowd two pairs of eyes must be affectionately watching his every move. His old mother was doing her best not to miss his slightest gesture, while his beautiful armor must be be dazzling the most bewitching eyes of the whole region with its bright gleam.

The governor waited for silence to be restored and then spoke:

My dear people, my dear children:

As every year, at this same time, I have called you together in order to inform you of the desires of our dearly beloved God: the Sacred Spider.

The audience was becoming more and more impatient but the governor seemed to pay little heed. He related, in minute detail, his embassy. And to begin with, the ritual of offerings and of purification, thanks to which he had prepared himself to encounter the face of the god.

He spared them no detail: the three nights of prayer and fasting in the mausoleum; the psalmodic procession he had led out to the Turtles' Oued; the offerings that he had deposited there; the return to the mausoleum; the ritual sacrifice of a black ram, a red rooster, and a white heifer at the foot of the ancient mulberry tree; the details of his lonely expedition through the labyrinth of valleys to the secret center of the Sacred Mountain; finally the miraculous meeting with the tutelary god.

"Our beloved God demands, as he does every year, half the harvest and a young virgin. This year the chosen virgin is . . ."

The Cracks in Time

They had not slept, they remained awake,
heaving great moans that welled up from
their breasts and from their entrails, as they
awaited daybreak on bended knees.

—The Popol-Vuh

It had begun just like any ordinary revolt of uncivilized, barefoot paupers, poor souls wasted from hard labor and merciless treatment, miserable underfed creatures.

Still, the plantations had grown quite green, watered with the blood and the sweat of the workers, and predictions for the year's harvests were exceptionally good. The *qadi* had been making more frequent visits out to his lands, leaving several overworked assistants to deal with the problems that would inevitably arise in his jurisdictions during his absence. He would return to Baghdad only to attend the rare meetings of the Diwan, which assembled around the caliph or his vizier all of the dignitaries in the empire.

And then one day, in the middle of the fields, a skirmish broke out between the guards and some seasonal workers. The insurgents massacred three militiamen, burned down a barn, and then fled in the direction of the salt marshes.

41

The *qadi,* momentarily disconcerted by this rebellion, quickly regained his composure: he dispatched a messenger to his friend the vizier, who immediately sent him a squadron of hardened soldiers. The sole sight of them was enough to reestablish order in the plantations, and work on the harvest was taken up again with renewed zeal. The *qadi* did not deem it necessary to pursue the group of renegades that the salt marshes, he hadn't the slightest doubt, would manage to finish off. Hunger and thirst would exterminate them, down to the very last man.

It wasn't until after the fourth disappearance that the *qadi* began to grow alarmed. Within the last two days, four workers had taken advantage of the cover of night to disappear from their place of work. The searches undertaken to find them remained fruitless. Facts had to be faced: the four men could only have disappeared by penetrating into the salt marshes, probably in search of the first group of renegades.

The *qadi* reinforced night surveillance of the garrets that served as dormitories for the weary workers. And everything seemed to return to normal. For several days, not one disappearance was reported and the harvest heaped in the bulging barns.

The disappearances started up again and the *qadi* was quite disturbed over it. He doubled the night watch, acquired specially trained dogs, had new fences put up. But nothing was of any use. The workers continued to desert his lands. And so he decided to approach the problem from another angle. He mobilized certain militiamen to act not as guards to stop this hemorrhage but rather as recruiting officers whose mission it was to provide day-to-day replacements for each post left vacant.

This was a wise and profitable solution for the *qadi*. Henceforward he paid no heed to the number of disappearances that were brought to his attention every morning and was only interested in knowing if a replacement was ready to fill the vacant post. For this reason, he was not unduly upset when the news reached him that other disappearances had occurred in neighboring domains. He was even so good-hearted as to call together the landowners of the region and encourage them to adopt the solution that he had conceived and that had served him so well, ridding him even of the need to bother about ensuring security on his lands. In fact, why should they force these miserable wretches to do work they didn't want to do, when the region was literally swarming with empty stomachs? For each worker who disappeared, a hundred others were willing to take up the task. One had but to dip into that vast reserve of idle arms. As for those who disappeared, the salt marshes would take care of them well enough.

That is how the *qadi* gained the reputation of being a very good and peaceful man, and even qualified as a great democrat.

An emergency meeting of the Diwan was called. The news was enough to seriously unsettle the powers-that-be: the salt marshes had not accomplished their work of death. The rebel renegades had been able — no one knows by what means — to cross them and to settle on the other side, on unexplored but, to all appearances, productive land.

There was even a rumor going around that they had begun to build a town that they called Al-Moukhtara (The Chosen, or The Elect), to organize community life, and to develop a system of administration. They had even chosen a leader, a man by the name of Rafik, a converted Nestorian who had been a brilliant student at the faculty of Philosophy and, according to the reports of the secret police, a disciple of certain corrupt philosophers, corrupters of the empire's young people. Certain members of the Diwan believed that a correlation could be drawn between the influence of these false masters' thinking and the concretization that, as the chosen name of the mutineer town attested, the disciple who had strayed into the midst of the renegades seemed to give to the utopic teachings he had received at the University, now happily brought back under control. For two long hours, the Diwan, effectively presided over by the caliph, debated the question.

First of all, the possibility of an armed intervention against the new city was envisaged. The idea was renounced after having gone once around the table. Not that anyone doubted that this was the ideal solution, but the war that was drawing out on the northern borders of the empire had mobilized the greater part of the troops, and everyone felt it would be particularly dangerous to send the capital's garrison—the essential guarantee of order in the city—out across the salt marshes on a punitive expedition, several days' march away from the city ramparts.

The Diwan adopted the point of view of the vizier, who advocated deferring any action in order to collect the greatest amount of useful information about the plans and the nature of the inhabitants of this city, sprung from the white fog of the salt marshes, by means of reports soon to be drafted by the information service's most cunning spies, who were to be sent on a mission without further delay, cleverly disguised as rebel workers. Then, after having studied the reports, they would determine the proper posture to strike. The Diwan dispersed after having adopted this wise tactic.

Out across the salt marshes, day-to-day life was being organized. The city was taking shape, due to the concerted efforts of two talented architects who had joined, almost simultaneously, the isolated colony, and the skilful artisans (stone-layers, *zelidjiers* (ceramists), carpenters) who had, little by little, come to swell the ranks of the first renegades.

A Council had been elected, and Rafik had been named to preside over it. The Council had set about drawing up a Contract that would serve as the basis for life in the social context of the new republic of Zanj (named in honor of the founders who consisted mainly of men and women of the black race). The foundations of community life were ruled by the principle of direct democracy. The administrative or decision-making bodies were all elected and everyone could aspire to eligibility, without distinction of race, sex, or belief. The possession of private property was altogether abolished.

The news coming from Al Moukhtara, through the agency of the dispatched spies, had at first disconcerted the Diwan, which after some time had been once again convened by the caliph. Instead of the disintegration that each of the members of the high jurisdiction had hoped for, the reports mentioned an undeniable consolidation of the community of paupers. Social organization, though based upon totally aberrant principles, seemed to have succeeded. Collective life in the city of renegades did not seem to raise any significant problems. The Minister of Justice even called attention to the fact that the reports made no mention of a crime rate. Was this an omission or an observation? The question was worth looking into.

The problem that the creation of the new city presented was becoming rather worrisome. For if the secret information which the Diwan had at its disposal were made public, wasn't there a risk of seeing this experiment exert a dangerous power of attraction upon easily impressionable souls? It was urgently necessary to prevent the information about the community of the Zanj from being broadcast.

But was this essentially defensive measure still satisfactory in the face of a danger that grew more evident day by day? It was true, the reports of the spies made no mention of any aggressive intentions on the part of the inhabitants of Al-Moukhtara. Hadn't they unanimously adopted their leader's proposition not to create a police force, or even the beginnings of an army, but only to organize a voluntary militia exclusively reserved for the defense of the city?

And besides, with this war on the borders dragging on, armed intervention still remained an impossibility.

The discussion was going around in circles, making no notable progress. The vizier put an end to the exchanging of points of view and proposed a solution.

Just as the worm corrupts the fruit, he suggested that they undermine from within the futile dream of these scatterbrains. Consequently, he recommended they liberate a few prisoners, chosen among the most hardened criminals and send them, like a Greek gift, to the rebel city. We would then see how fine ideals fall apart and how the most noble enterprises are toppled.

The idea having filled the assembly with admiration, it was adopted immediately; the vizier's subtlety was unanimously applauded.

When the first releases were made, the prisoners did not know to whom or to what they owed this unexpected leniency! First of all, a group of ten prisoners, among the most dangerous, were safely escorted out to the edge of the salt marshes. During the night, the guards relaxed their vigilance and the prisoners disappeared into the fog that floated continually over the salty stretch of land. After that, other groups were set free in the same way, out into the wilderness.

After long days of thirsty walking, they all made their way to the city that—rumors had vaguely hinted —rebel workers had founded on the other side of the salt marshes.

When the first group of released prisoners showed up at the foot of the ramparts, the Council of the Zanj was convened to deliberate upon the way in which to deal with these little-desired new recruits. Despite a certain amount of mistrust on the part of a few of the members, Rafik succeeded in having his point of view adopted: prison was a punishment which had never solved any problems. Delinquency and criminality were, in his opinion, diseases that required healing, not repression. Consequently, he was for giving these new-comers a chance by integrating them into the society, providing them with work and with leisure activities, and by considering them as men who could be reha-bilitated without question.

The inhabitants of Al-Moukhtara, assembled in the agora, adopted, after long discussions, the propositions of the Council and the gates of the city opened before the haggard prisoners.

The vizier was seriously concerned. The results of his stratagem in no way coincided with what he had reckoned on. No disorder had actually perturbed the organization of the renegade city after the integration of released prisoners. At most, in the beginning, there had been a few small disturbances. But very quickly order had been restored and, it was plain to see, the dangerous delinquents were in the process of redeeming themselves with conduct that was increasingly respectable! That which the caliph's prisons had not succeeded in accomplishing, the bold and crazy venture of an illuminated utopist was achieving: the redemption and the integration of criminals who had been thought forever lost to the community!

The vizier was deeply perplexed at these findings. He disregarded the affairs of State and closed himself up in his study. A solution had to be found as quickly as possible, for if this danger persisted, it would soon undermine the very foundations of the world that meant so much to him: a world of order built upon natural hierarchies (could they be reasonably denied?) and organized to combat the baseness and evil that characterize human nature in order to maintain the elements of civilization that the stronger and more naturally gifted beings had succeeded in extricating from the dangerous collective vertigo of temptation, endlessly perpetuated by the fluctuations of the sheep-like herd, the instinct of self-destruction, and the void.

Yes, there must be a solution. He had quite a few volumes brought to him from his library and closed the door to all petitions.

In the soft twilight that was descending upon Al-Moukhtara, Rafik was thinking about his old master who had the misfortune of dying without seeing his dream materialize. How proud he would have been to see the work of his disciple, a work entirely inspired by his teachings and one that inflicted upon his most vehement critics a scathing and concrete challenge.

After seven days, the vizier emerged from his study. He took up his everyday activities once again. A strange smile lit his face. He believed he had found the solution. His mistake had been in releasing criminals, hardened, to be sure, but with absolutely no political or ethical convictions. Having read the ancient masters had edified him. Revolutions only die from the lack of a coherent and rigorously defined political program or, inversely, from surpassing their proper norms. His idea to send, into the midst of the city, elements to corrupt it from within was still valid (the blind bard related the tale of Ulysses' ingenious strategy which allowed Agamemnon to triumph over the prideful Troy). He had only to change agents in order to hasten the downfall. He was going to stick into the belly of his imaginary horse everything that Baghdad could muster of rigid ideologists, maximalist philosophers, and stray prophets. Their teachings would bring about the upheaval that the unarmed criminals had been unable to instigate.

Mahdi had been arrested and very rapidly accused of heresy and blasphemy. His trial had been conducted expeditiously and the death sentence pronounced had not aroused any protestation, even among the worst heretics on record with the secret police. It was that his line of thinking did not fit in with any other form of heresy known to that day.

He had begun his notorious career of irreverent preacher with a few very artless eccentricities.

A wealthy merchant, he had enjoyed the general respect of everyone and lived a quiet life, although tainted with a certain immorality. The receptions he organized in his luxurious household were ill-famed. The free-thinking philosophers and the Bacchic poets, his most loyal friends, were assembled on these occasions, along with the dregs of society: known street-walkers, young lads of lax morals, female singers as highly reputed for the beauty of their voices as for the permissiveness of their conduct. And the wine would flow abundantly. Then suddenly, one day he left everything behind and went to seek refuge up in the mountains. He returned after nine months of voluntary reclusion, emaciated, cloaked in a large tunic of coarse cloth, a long greying beard hiding his face, and with the disturbing gleam of the illuminated in his eyes. It was then, roaming through the streets of the city, heedless of the insults and the stones that children hurled at him, that he began his preaching:

"Verily, I say unto you: No prophet should suffer the unjust fate of seeing his message altered to meet the requirements of the powers-that-be. For then, the divine messenger who mocks time, might, under the circumstances, become legislator, accountable for the strife and the vain quarrels of the tribe. For then his eyes, dimmed, no longer fix their sights upon the infinity of the horizon, his ears, deafened, no longer listen to the vast sound of the Eternal, and his body, chastened, is no longer able to receive, in fear and trembling, the presence of the God of Light.

"No Sacred Book can be perverted in its consubstantial truth to the point of becoming a code for the use of the legislators of the earthly city.

"Know how to be discerning in consulting it. Track down relentlessly the wrong application of Truth and its enslavement to the norms of the time or to the malefic scheme of the powerful.

"Do you believe, oh credulous ones, that a messenger from God need trouble himself with the prohibition of drink, the codification of the laws of marriage, or of succession, and that in the name of his message your lives can be regimented, your aspirations plotted and evaluated, your desires closed up in a blind prison of every imaginable frustration?

"Verily, I say unto you, of sole import are the Inspiration and the Light, the Questioning and the Quest.

"Look upon the infinity of sidereal space, meditate upon the mysteries of the Eternal Return, reflect upon what becomes of the soul, and venture forth, bold diviners of the Absolute, beyond the gates of death.

"These alone are the eternal questions that merit the mediation of a messenger of God!

"All the rest is imposture. . . ."

Despite the gravity of these deviationist and unorthodox remarks, the authorities had at first more or less tolerated the irreverent ravings of the blasphemous mystic, the heretic sufi *zindiq*.

But there came a time when his outbursts became inadmissible, for public order was threatened by the calls to revolt that the unconscious madman put forth:

"Do you not see that social codification set up as an inalterable dogma is a masquerade? Are the laws that were enacted in Ancient Times to resolve particular difficulties of the time adapted to the complex needs of our time? What do they have to do with the spiritual message anyway, a message that in itself transcends the fluctuations of History? Do you not see that the confusion that is maintained between the spiritual substance of revelation and the chance and profane crumbs of the legislator has ended in firmly seating the seat of power and justifying all injustice, in passing off the shadow for the prey, and in confusing the aleatory with the essential, just as in the 'Khayal al Dhil,' in which the puppets fade into the background leaving only their shadows in the hands of a showman, a master of illusion.

"Verily I say unto you, the time of lucidity has come . . ."

It was to prevent him from further disseminating his disquieting doctrine that the vizier issued the order to arrest and incarcerate Mahdi. And now the vizier was congratulating himself for not having too hastily signed the decree to implement the death penalty, the appropriate punishment for the illuminated madman that had been recommended by the emergency court. He was convinced that Mahdi was to play a first-hand role in his undertaking. That very night, Mahdi was released and escorted out to the edges of the salt marshes. Without a word, the guards left him. And he made his way through the mists in the direction of the city of hope.

Mahdi's arrival in Al-Moukhtara was followed by that of other respected philosophers and preachers. At first, Rafik and the Council welcomed these unexpected appearances with much solicitude and joy. They were honored to see the freest thinkers of their time join their community.

But quite soon problems arose that greatly sobered their initial reaction. The preachers surrounded themselves with disciples. Their divergent teachings soon set the circles of their respective followers against one another. At first, everything was done in a healthy and pacific manner: they debated nonstop about the imagined or nonimagined nature of the Koran. Some, free disciples of Mo'tazila (a school of rational thought) defended materialism; other mystics of different faiths retaliated in the name of idealism.

Afterward, the clans grouped together into exclusive cliques. The first criticisms against the Council came from the libertarians. They put into question the very legitimacy of such a body. For them, all power, regardless of the mask it assumed, was in its very essence pernicious and reductive. Their teachings spread with lightning speed. The day came when Rafik, their primary target, had to confront attacks from their adherents within the Council itself. In vain he argued that what mattered for him was the administration of things, and not the government of men; he found himself in the minority and was forced to step down from his office. Other elements found their way into the Council, which stood its ground in spite of the criticisms of the libertarians and even consolidated its power. The population of Al-Moukhtara, frightened of the libertarian doctrines and their provocations (a field had been burned and many herd animals slaughtered by uncontrollable members of the libertarian party) had, during an emergency meeting of the general assembly, widened the powers of the Council. Another party was soon formed. It called itself the World Revolution Party. Its followers believed that the revolution should be exported outside the city walls, and carried, first of all, into the very heart of Baghdad by means of a military intervention. Strategists underlined the fact that advantage must be taken of the exceptional circumstances that then prevailed, but that could not last forever: Had not the war on the northern borders stationed the greater part of the Caliphate's troops far from Baghdad? This new party met with great success and won the elections. Hastily, armed forces were mustered and feverish preparations were made for the triumph over the empire's capital city.

Excerpts from Rafik's private diary

> Why is it that the most promising flowers molder? Why do revolutions die? Undoubtedly because we continue to hold a sacred view of politics.

How can we change the world and man if we continue to accept, by simply inverting them, the rules of the game established by our adversaries, and if we are satisfied with replacing the Caliphate with a centralized and dogmatic State designed for reigning over shadows . . . for their own well-being?

No hope of real change is possible without making radical breaks away from our very way of thinking. Tomorrow civil society should take the lead over the machinery of State and politics will no longer be the simple conquest of power, but the organization of debates and struggles centered around the exercise of responsibilities and administrative duties.

The Diwan, summoned upon the announcement of the imminent attack, developed a defense strategy. The serene attitude of the vizier bolstered confidence. And everyone prepared for the confrontation.

The debacle of the assailing army was complete. The retreating troops were pursued all the way back to the ramparts of Al-Moukhtara, which was besieged. The inhabitants were put to death by the sword and not a single edifice survived the destruction.

Rafik, mortally wounded, dragged himself over to a thorn bush at the edge of a clearing. He hid there and awaited death. In the mists that enveloped the sweeping desolation, a misshapen figure appeared holding fast to his mount. He knew that it was the Man on the Donkey, who would soon attack Mahdia, the Fatimid capital, and that his soul, on the verge of leaving him, would be reincarnated in this miserable body in order to continue his unfinished work.

He died peacefully, for a sign had appeared to him that he had interpreted as proof that revolutions often fail, but that they never die.

The Navigator was spellbound. The stories about power had deeply affected him. He had listened to them attentively, ever more avidly; and still, as each one drew to its close there lingered, deep in his knotted throat, a taste of ashes . . .

The Astrolabe could sense his excitement and his bitterness. And so, as if to comfort him, it began to tell him a few other stories . . .

Reflections

The greatest separation of all: when our bodies are united.

—Al Mutanabbi

O, Indira, your nudity is the omega of the world, your dance its lyrical offering. For you the goddess Sarasvati plays eternally upon her vina. The gentle poet Alauddin Khije, reborn from his ashes, accompanies her with his sitar, while the beating of my heart mingles with the muted and insane percussion of a blind musician beating upon his mad mridangam.

Ragas of the evening and of the morning.

Indira, may your immodest laughter ring out again and forever.

From my entire glass surface I reflect you.

I would love to multiply your fiery image to infinity. Ah!

I am a drunken prism, I am the kinetic obsession, fervor and frigidity, erection and deliquescence, desire and impotence.

The Ganges flows through Benares.
Its course is immutable.
Flea-infested fakirs and flaccid skeletons

61

Splash in its troubled waters
Then go some few meters off
To die of hunger.

A high-angle shot, through an open roof:
A woman is dancing before a mirror.
The fire crackles in the hearth.
Hindu figurines blush slightly
Is it because of the fire-flush or
The lasciviousness of the dance?

Off to the land of the Tarahumaras
Flee
Never stopping
Here are the docks
Masts crucifying the sky
And drawing pearls of red upon its darkened brow
The waning stars.
Blow out your sail, O my frigate
Mayflower of all perdition.
Fly, yes fly
Upon your mizzenmast
Banner of my fervor.

Indira, I delight in your regal immodesty, the
extravagance of your appetite and the masterful archi-
tecture that you unceasingly invent for the bodies intertwining in ardent rapture between your sheets. My icy
gaze is witness to all your turpitude, to all the delirious
ecstasies you inspire.

Placid, I admire you Indira, lovable harlot, you apply conscientiously the sacred teachings of the Kamasutra. And you know, my sweet corruption, when you raise your smooth firm breasts up so nice and high, golden apples of the Garden of the Hesperides, when you enclose the male principle within your incandescent ovaries, yes, you know that I, mirrored surface, the stretch of asexuality, burn for you with all the fires of damnation.

When, after your ecstasy, you contemplate in me your triumphant nudity, I have, more than once, caught the perverse look in your eyes taunting and making of me your conspirator.

Queen of vice, O my demented one, you know well, you who believes in metempsychosis, that, in my whole mirror soul, I am jealous.

And yet I again implore you: May your immodest laughter forever ring out, for your nudity is the omega of the world.

For ages, she walked through the wind and the mist, Lalded, the Great-Mother, the ancestor. And her laughter was defiance and her ascetic nudity sang the glory of Shiva.

She fled the armies of Sayyïd Ali of Hamdan, the conqueror, and the valleys resounded with her song.

She went up to the mountain and spoke with the Master.

Since then six centuries have passed on the trees throughout Kashmir. Her quatrains, caught up in the topmost branches, scintillate, iridescent dewdrops, for each newborn day.

> *My Master said but one thing to me:*
> *From without, said he, go within*
> *This has become for me magical formula and prophecy*
> *And thus I began to dance in the nude.*

Oh! hear me
Avidly take in the translucent seeds, sown
for you by the drunken ascetic
Keep always your logical desperation.
Tenderly nurse your horrid blasphemies.
Be ever more
The restive mule, the perverse temptation,
The inviolable refusal.
At your footsteps would that the blazes of
Liberation forever burst forth! Be the insatiable devourer.
O Indira carnivorous flower
No prey in itself is worthy of your slow swallowing
Nor your honeyed and fragrant juices
Nor this death-life that you impart with each embrace.

> *The universe seems honest to honest men for their eyes have been blindfolded. That is why they feel no anxiety at hearing the crowing of the cock or upon discovering a star-filled sky.*
> —Georges Bataille

The morning after nightlong loving
Feverishly the official who had gained the favors
of the cover girl felt as
spirited as a schoolboy.
He asked her to marry him.
At first she laughed at such a proposal
Was even offended, but she did not say no . . .

O Indira, what dark premonitions!
That very morning, you gazed long into me at
yourself
And you were not naked and your body draped in
the sari
Was docile. And your eyes heavy and so distracted.

The first wrinkles . . . why
Must the flesh betray?
The official is charming . . . but
Can I assume a normalized life?

She accepted my proposal.
She will be mine, all mine.
O what joy, yes but I must make
My family accept this marriage.

The future mother-in-law to her youngster:
"I advise you against this exotic thing:
You know quite well that
Oriental spices never agreed with you."

The die has been cast, I'll try to get accustomed
to the smell of the kitchens.

Judas
Vile traitress
You have betrayed us: your refusals, your blas-
phemies, my ecstasies
and my torment
Soon you will go toward your fate of Sundays with
the family.
Of departmental prittle-prattle, of perorations, of
preachiness,
Of dishcloths, of divans, of clothing
Respectability, of marital duties nobly fulfilled to
ensure
The survival of the species
Disgusting!

Before leaving her studio, the
Cover girl, undressing slowly
Performs before her mirror a
Hieratical and violent dance.
The last. The farewell dance.
The statues blush. The drum
Beats against her flanks frantically . . .

Here you are back again. Dance my love and may
your immodest laughter forever ring out. Would that
we never part again. Dance. Dance. Dance. I am a
drunken prism, I am the kinetic obsession, fervor and

frigidity, erection and deliquescence, desire and impotence. . . . Dance, dance dance.

Ah! I shall burst . . .

Read in the miscellaneous column:

> Last night, an incredible accident cost the life of a well known cover girl. She was literally stabbed to death in her studio by the fragments of glass from a full-length standing mirror which suddenly shattered. She was found, lying on the floor, completely naked.

There are four schools of dance in India: the bharata natyam of Thanjavur, the khathakali of Malabar, the kathak from the North, and the manipuri from the East. Which of these dances was the cover girl performing when she was stabbed to death by the thousands of shattered fragments of glass?

Indira. Your nudity is forever the omega of the world.

Thar

Off with you, fly, I am pregnant with my lord.
— Proverb from the Atlas Mountains

When the sun sank all the way down to the horizon, the lost horseman spurred his steed, rashly urging it on, beyond its limits.

The young man was shaking with fear and yet, he had shown it many times over, he was no coward. But ever since the strange disappearances that had suddenly begun to occur in the region and which continued to decimate the males of his tribe, the Banou Rabias, he knew how dangerous it was to lose one's way in this deserted immensity of the Rob Khali, which the panicked imagination of his tribe now populated with giant bats, evil ogres, and voracious succubi.

As far as he was concerned, he had never really believed in that nonsense. But the systematic disappearance of a number of his tribesmen was an undeniable fact and no obvious and irrefutable explanation had been proposed up to now. These strange disappearances had begun one year after the close of an incident quite widely talked about at the time when he himself was still but a boisterous young boy. He could, nevertheless, recall every detail about it.

69

In the beginning it had been a stupid matter of jealousy.

The beautiful Aïcha Kandicha of the Kalb tribe, their ally, had a number of suitors, but the true contest was between her own cousin and the son of the chieftain of the Banou Rabias. She chose her cousin and their marriage sealed a long and beautiful love story. The rejected candidate then conceived an undying hatred.

Seven days after the celebration of the marriage, the two former rivals met along with a few friends for the agapes, in which the glasses were kept well-filled. The drink accomplished its evil deed and soon the two drunken men began to quarrel. A confused fight ensued. The two adversaries were separated, but one of them slumped suddenly to the ground. The husband of the beautiful Aïcha Kandicha would never rise again. A severe blow to the temple had killed him instantly. Aïcha Kandicha, mad with grief, did not weep, barely even allowed a whimper to escape, but demanded that the law of retaliation be applied.

The two chieftains met and discussed the matter at length. Strategic imperatives made it impossible to allow their alliance (utterly indispensable, considering the maneuvres of the enemy tribes led by the Banou Chaddad) to be broken because of an unfortunate accident.

So they decided to apply the customary laws, which in certain cases allowed for the waiving of the ancient blood law. It was agreed that the tribe of Banou Rabias would grant to the family of the unhappy victim one thousand white camels and a herd of one hundred sheep, in reparation for damages incurred. This arrangement was accepted by everyone excepting the widow, who continued for three days to demand, resolutely, the application of the ancient law. None of the steps taken to bring her to change her mind succeeded in swaying her determination. Having run out of arguments, the Chief of the Kalbs advised her parents to leave her be, convinced that time would work its charm, and that forgetting would heal the wounds.

It was on the fourth day after the agreement between the two chieftains had been concluded that Aïcha Kandicha's disappearance was noticed.

They found in her tent all the possessions that she had not deemed necessary to take along and, pinned to the center post, a blood-stained piece of white cloth on which was written in red letters, simply one word, THAR (revenge). Everyone believed that Aïcha Kandicha, mad with grief, had slit her wrists, and, after having written this word in her own blood, had wandered away from the camp. The chief of the tribe ordered beaters out into the bush to find and bring back the demented girl before she bled to death. Suicide was strictly forbidden, for it could only bring misfortune and damnation upon the tribe. The scattered bloodstains were followed. But soon the stains suddenly stopped, without any apparent explanation. The searches lasted for seven days. The immediate surroundings of the camp were minutely explored, all escarpments were searched, no shelter likely to serve as a hiding place or as a grave was neglected. The searches were extended all the way out to the limits of the pasturelands. In vain. One was forced to simply accept the enigma: Aïcha Kandicha seemed to have literally disappeared into thin air.

The searches were abandoned and it was forbidden to invoke the name of the mysterious missing girl so as not to bring down upon the tribe the ire of the al-Lata, Manat, and al Ozza divinities, who would not fail to take offense at the impious act. (Even though nothing concrete ever turned up to prove its veracity, this conclusion was the only plausible explanation for the disappearance of the inconsolable widow.)

Little by little, the members of the two allied tribes began to forget the regrettable incident that had nearly caused their alliance to fail and the puzzling disappearance of the widow ceased to trouble people's minds.

But exactly one year after the unfortunate day upon which Aïcha Kandicha's husband had died, a strange event took place that caused old fears to crop up again: the tribe awaited, in vain, the return of the son of the chief of the Banou Rabias, gone out unescorted across the desert of Rob Khali. All searches remained fruitless and nothing could be done but simply take note of his mysterious disappearance.

Ever since then, no man from the Banou Rabia tribe who had incautiously strayed into the Rob Khali, had ever come back alive and not the slightest trace of the missing men could ever be found by the numerous expeditions organized to that effect.

The sun was now disappearing behind the small hills and darkness was beginning to spread behind the shivering back of the lost horseman. Fear gripped him and he no longer even thought of keeping it from showing. He had been desperately searching the horizon for some time when, from behind a hillock, he caught sight of the vague glimmer of a tiny campfire. He turned his horse in that direction. "Finally! Someone to keep me company. We'll spend the night together and then tomorrow, just before daybreak, we'll start out again. Perhaps he knows the trails better than I do." He had gotten within a few strides of the fire and could now clearly make out the silhouette of his future fellow traveler, who, muffled up in a fine burnoose, was turning his back to him.

Drawing his horse to a halt, he jumped to the ground and walked over to the fire. The burnoose pivoted, and the fair face of its bearer was revealed to him. It was a young man of great beauty and his huge eyes shone magnificently.

Under the gaze of those eyes, the horseman felt as if he were spellbound. He responded automatically to the traditional salutations and recounted the tale of his wanderings in a monotone voice. The young man reassured him and invited the horseman to accompany him to a cavern he knew of, where they might find shelter for the night. Tomorrow they would travel on together.

The horseman felt a strange languor running through all of his limbs, and he docilely followed the young man walking away ahead of him. They rapidly came upon a heap of rocks. The young man walked over to a bush, pulled it toward himself, and an opening appeared between two rocks. He disappeared into it and the horseman followed without hesitating.

The scene that met his eyes dumbfounded him and yet he accepted everything that was happening to him with incredible detachment. They were in the entryway to a huge cavern brightly lit with reflections bouncing off a multitude of mirrors that covered the walls. A double row of statues (or could they really be stark-naked, wide-eyed men with frosty white hair?) stretched from one end of the cavern to the other.

The horseman silently followed the young man. In the mirrors, it seemed to him that their shadows were very tenuous.

Finally, they reached the other end of the cavern.

Exquisite notes of music and delicious smells of food aroused his fatigue and his hunger. The young man drew back an embroidered silk curtain and they entered a marvelously decorated room. The horseman admired the lovely pool in its center, inlaid with blue and green ceramic tile, and he saw that the musical notes were emitted by a series of instruments: a mother-of-pearl lute, an intricately wrought *kanoun,* and a polished *rebab,* which not a single hand stroked, but which were giving forth a sweet music on their own. His eye was drawn to the low table creaking under the weight of already prepared victuals and wine-filled glasses. With a wave of the arm, the young man enjoined him to bathe, then he disappeared without a word behind a tapestry that hid (the horseman had just time enough to glimpse it) a deep, low bed.

He shed his clothing mechanically, and descended the stairs of the sunken bath. With its liquid caress, water enveloped his body, which ached from the travails of his journey.

It was just as he was beginning to drop off to sleep in the water that She appeared, drawing back the tapestry behind which his young companion had disappeared a few moments earlier. Never in his life had he seen such a seductive creature. Entirely naked, she joined him in the bath, and the welcoming water lapped voluptuously about her. They bathed together, and the horseman could feel desire mounting within him. But, flirting, she eschewed his embrace and proposed that he first satisfy his stomach. To the sound of the music played by the invisible orchestra, they gave themselves over to a feast, copiously washed down with wine.

Afterwards, it was she who, pulling him by the hand, took the initiative to draw him over to the foot of the bed he had glimpsed behind the tapestry that had made possible the metamorphosis about which he could no longer even feel astonished.

There, overwhelmed by the violence of his desire, he wanted to take her in haste. But she pushed him away and, spreading her thighs, revealed her vulva, from which the lost horseman saw fly a myriad of multi-colored butterflies.

Feverish with excitement, he could not dwell upon

the feeling of amazement that the supernatural flight had inspired in him. He drew the beauty inexorably toward him and covered her. The whirling of colored wings thinned slowly above the intertwining bodies . . .

That night the horseman knew transports of ecstasy he had never dared dream of, accustomed as he was to the coarse lovemaking of desert women.

Everything was new to him and so very exciting that he lost count of his orgasms. Drained, his body numbed, he sank down onto the bed, enfolded the beauty in his amorous arms, and allowed himself to slip off into an irresistible sleep.

It was a cold breeze that bit into his skin, awakening him. He sensed an insurmountable weakness all through his body and could distinctly feel a painful throbbing at his neck. Up above in the sky, the stars grew pale, and the twins of Gemini drew apart. He had the physical sensation of living the very same dissociation and he stared down at the wan body, drained of its blood, sprawled out in his place on the bed where he had known such voluptuousness. He could see on the neck of the body that had been his own, the very clear mark of the incisors that had ripped open the skin to suck out all the blood.

The body, which was on the verge of departing from life, had just the strength to lift its eyelids and he realized that he was lovingly embracing a skeleton crawling with fetid worms.

He then knew, before slipping definitively into unconsciousness, that Aïcha Kandicha would add a new statue—trunk-man in a petrified forest—to her collection lined up in the hall of mirrors and that the implacable malediction, cast upon the men of his tribe, would not end until the vengeance of the succuba had no more subjects upon which to practice.

"What is speech?"
"It is a passing wind."
"And who can fetter it?"
"The written word."

Thus responded Al Qualquachandi to the questions of his disciple.

"Allow me now, Friend, to speak to you of the torment and of the splendor of creation, said the Astrolabe. Come, listen to the story of the adventurous deed of a few sowers of stars. . . ."

The Two Calligraphers

I want a heart that is torn by exile
So that I may tell it of the pain of desire.

—Jelaluddin Rumi

Are not words and meaning, the rainbows
and illusory bridges cast between beings who
are forever separate?

—Nietzsche

The Calligrapher cast a rapid glance over his work of the day before, took off his burnoose, and sat down at his worktable. With his left hand, he instinctively tidied a few objects that were lying about and began to do something with his right arm, but stopped immediately. His eyes dropped to the stump that now took the place of his right forearm, and a wave of melancholy flooded through him.

He thought back to the days of his glory. At that time he had been the head scribe of the palace and the caliph treated him with respect and courtesy. But most important, he had been the official calligrapher for his friends: the free-thinking philosophers of the Mo'tazila, to whose friendship he owed so many discoveries, and the existential Bacchic poets, from whom he had learned to apprehend and feel, in every fiber of his soul, the frailty and the miracle of life.

Once, even the greatest painter of the time, Yahia Ibn Mahmoud Al-Wasiti, deigned to combine his talent with his own and they produced a fine hybrid work in service of the Maquamats de Hariri. But what he was most proud of in his life would always be the fact that in spite of all the temptations and sometimes even the threats, he had never agreed to prostitute his art by consenting to serve casuistic grammarians, fanatic theologians, or opportunistic shysters in general. His obstinate refusals had even brought down upon him the lasting hatred of the party for law and order.

Then the times had changed. The caliph, weakened with age, had fallen prey to the finagling of the guardians of the faith. The emancipating philosophers were thrown into prison, the poets banished, and the prose writers duly censured. Even the great Ghazali, who had proclaimed in the fervor of his youth that doubt was the foundation of knowledge and of being (was it not one of the sources of his legitimate pride to have been the inspired copyist of that text?) changed his tone and cruelly derided his former colleagues in his commentary on the Tahafut-al-Falasifa, that act of recreancy. He himself, in those times of decadence and regression, had had his hand cut off for having dared to copy a forbidden text by the great Jahiz: "The Epistle on the quarrel between the traders of male and female slaves." He owed his life, in fact, to having fled into this desolate, semi-desert region where, until the day he died, he had the intention of saving from destruction and obscurity texts that had now been relegated to the hell of private libraries and promised to the flame if they were ever discovered by the spies of the infamous new vizier.

The Calligrapher sighed deeply, shook himself to his senses. His daydreams fell away from him like scales of old skin sloughed off. He took up the calamus, his reed pen, in his left hand, which it had taken three years to re-educate so it might replace the right one, now probably reduced to bits of cartilage strewn about here and there in the dark corners of the cell, his torture chamber.

He dipped the end of his pen into the inkwell and began to trace the first lines of the text he had chosen to copy on that day.

The Drunken Mystic

The wise man can laugh only with a tremble.
—An Arab proverb

"That day, Dean Salcheddine Açafadi was finding it most difficult to concentrate on his lecture. His wandering imagination offered him glimpses of the delightful evening, which was so long in coming. He had invited every lofty intellectual, inspired mystic, Bacchic poet, and reputed professor in all of Baghdad to honor the residence that had just been put at his disposal as dean of the University and which constituted a whole wing of the magnificent architectural complex, including the Great Mosque, the administrative and technical quarters of the University, and the outbuildings for the domestics."

"The cooks were busying themselves with the preparation of succulent and aphrodisiac dishes, and the servants were finishing up the preparations to welcome the guests of the newly named dean in an appropriate fashion.

"The dignified professor stifled with great difficulty a sigh of impatience as he thought of the lovely bulging jars, of the crystalline cups. (Only old grouches and atrabilious crabs could contend that the Koran prohibited wine! He knew of two verses, at the least, with which to refute their troublesome readings!)

"He stoically continued to comment upon this *Lamia al Ajam,* which certain people found admirable, but which he himself found tedious and filled with empty and redundant platitudes.

Fingering his amber chaplet, the sheikh thought tenderly of old Kamaralzamane, his faithful procuress. He had insisted in his interview with her that she bring to his home, for this exceptional night, the most ravishing girls and the most handsome youths in the whole city so that he might honor his illustrious guests. At last the lecture was over and the dean, after having taken leave of his students, rushed off to his house. As rapidly as the dignity of his position would allow, he hurried down the corridors of the university, came out upon the interior courtyard of the Great Mosque, crossed it diagonally, opened the small communicating door, and found himself in the garden of his residence. He heaved a sigh, closed the door behind him, and began inspecting all the preparations for the reception.

"The evening had begun most auspiciously and continued to bode the best of omens. The old procuress had kept her word and the dean was very proud of the stunning maidens and handsome youths that cheered up the evening with their laughter and their pleasantly perverse games. The very greatest names had rallied to his call. The details of the evening had been perfectly orchestrated: the fare was delicious, the wines delicate, and the famous singer Oulaya had delighted her audience as much with the beauty of her voice as with the grace of her poems.

"The dean, greatly satisfied, was listening to the discussion which had opposed his two neighbors at the table. The learned Abu al-Qasim al-Ashari (the dean had never much liked him: he believed that he had a tendency to espouse dangerous dogmatisms. But, given his reputation, he had nevertheless been obliged to invite him) was denying any possibility of literary or artistic creation by arguing that the Koran was the fundament and the finality of all writing.

"Averröes (whose commentary on Plato's *Republic* the dean admired, and whose innovative and emancipating ideas he secretly upheld: he felt honored that this man, on a brief visit to Baghdad, had accepted his invitation) retorted cautiously that the original of the Koran was like a platonic model and that men, in their ethnic and historical diversity, could take it upon themselves to reformulate its tenets in their own particular and diversified fashions, which amounted, each time, to a creation.

"Abu Hayan al-Tawhidi (whom the dean considered, along with Ibn al-Arabi, to be the greatest thinker of the day) joined the discussion and eloquently defended the virtues of the creative and innovative interpretation of texts, even of sacred texts, and demonstrated irrefutably the dangers of all attitudes advocating repetitiousness or any exaggerated respect for dogma, no matter what the dogma might be.

(The calligrapher noted here that "The simultaneous presence of these great minds, in the same place at the same time, will set the majestic beards of learned historians and the steamy glasses of all credible thinkers to quivering. May they quiver . . .")

"Although he was keenly interested in the discussion, the dean decided that the time had come to impart a different ambience to the evening. Upon a sign from him, the servants refilled the wine glasses, and then, seating upon his knee a beautiful young woman who had disrobed and offered the splendor of her naked body to the whole assembly, he called for the fool Hassam and asked him to expound upon his joys and his pleasures for all the guests. The fool stepped forward, seated himself on the edge of the basin, and declared: 'These are my pleasures: walking about with no pants on amidst learned persons, picking quarrels with either sad or stupid persons, fleeing the company of vile persons . . .'

"A slightly tipsy grammarian dipped his beard into the wine and pulled over to him a beardless youth and a young girl stripped to the skin. He sat them both down in his lap and, kissing them each in turn, fondling them, he spoke to Hassam, 'Hassam, I beg of you, help me to resolve a dilemma. Who, between this sweet dove and this handsome starling, should I first honor with my attentions?' Hassam took on a theatrical posture and proclaimed, 'I can not settle the question until I have experimented for myself.'

"The guests clapped their hands in approval, 'Yes, yes, Hassam, experiment and light the way for our members!' A circle of spectators formed. They brought over the young woman and the young man, whom they undressed, and laid them down before Hassam, who without further hesitation began paying his respects to each of them in turn.

"When Hassam had finished his active comparison, he rose to his feet and was urged to arbitrate. He assumed an indignant look and sententiously declared, 'You have all lost your senses, how can you ask an honest man to compare two things that are incomparable? Did I officiate in the same receptacles?'

"Afterwards, he mischievously slipped away amid bursts of laughter and vague exclamations of protest. Then a poet stepped forward and pronounced:

Pour the wine, pour some more and still more.
Then tell me well: This is wine!
And do not have me drink in secret when

My consent is licit.
Cheating would be to see me full awake
And lucid.
For to me, stuttering and tottering,
The real trophy could be nothing but drunkenness

(Obviously the poet in question is the great Abu Nuwas.)

"The singer took up these same verses accompanying herself with her oud and voluptuous groups began to form. The intertwining of bodies created the most intricate of figures.

"The gold of time shone out then as brilliantly as a benediction.

"Some time passed; then from the midst of the languorous bodies a figure rose. The drunken mystic, stepping lightly, made his way toward a tall mirror leaning up against a column. He contemplated his shining mask in the surface of the glass. The guests, replete with drink and sensuality, stretched themselves and observed the apparition. With a very slow gesture, he began to remove his mask. But under the first mask, a second appeared. And so forth and so on, seven times over. The last mask removed, there appeared in place of a face, a dark hole in which was formed, in a whirling vortex, the compass rose.

"The bodies shivered in the icy blast, the drunken breath of the masked prophet.

"And in the milky light of dawn, a cock crowed . . ."

The Calligrapher stopped writing. He set down his refillable fountain pen on the edge of the embroidered desk pad he had acquired on a recent journey aboard an airplane that had carried him toward his destination, and he carefully rubbed his eyes with his fingertips. Their extreme fatigability was a constant source of alarm to him. He had attempted in vain to drive back into the recesses of unconsciousness the obvious facts: soon he would lose what little sight was left to him and he would have to resort to an assistant—a stenographer as they called them—to dictate what he could no longer transcribe in his small, pinched handwriting. His friend Victoria would help him find someone discreet and loyal, perhaps she would even be able to discover the rare gem among the personnel at the journal.

He stifled a sigh, then valiantly went back to work . . .

Terra incognita or the enigmatic portrait . . .

(Rough sketch to be developed.)

"Once upon a time there was a painter who was very highly reputed. He was coveted by the princes of his day, who showered him with gold to induce him to immortalize their features and their sumptuous courts. The great men of the world fought to obtain his favors and his fellow painters were jealous of his exceptional success.

"And yet the rare people who were close to him knew that he was not happy. Little impressed with fame or fortune, he continued to live in the modest home that his father had left him, and his solitary and taciturn temperament never faltered or changed. He lived a retired life, was only interested in his art, always dwelling upon the same obsession: to achieve, one day or another, the great work. A canvas that could contain, on its painted surface, like a trick mirror, the quintessence of truth, all of the marvels and mysteries of the earth, evidence itself.

"One day he sailed away on a ship and, leaving his acquired position and his honors, he adventurously explored foreign lands and seas.

"His jealous fellow painters carried on cruelly about his mad escapade. They made fun of his vainglory and his adventurism and they made jokes about the probable results of his wanderings, 'This will certainly bring us in a fine harvest of baboon portraits and superb landscapes of desolate stretches of desert.' But, silently, they rejoiced in this unexpected windfall and promised themselves to win the position, now vacant, of appointed portraitist to the princely courts.

"Meanwhile, the painter imperturbably traveled over the seas and feverishly collected sketches, notes, and illustrations of everything he saw.

"Seven years went by.

"Upon his return, he closed himself up in a stark room and devoted himself to assembling on a vast canvas the entirety of what he had brought back from his long odyssey. Everyone forgot about him, except one old servant who, every day at noon and in the evening, continued to set out before the locked door of the ascetic's studio the meager sustenance necessary to his survival.

"One day she saw that the dishes she had put there had not been touched. This aroused her curiosity, but she resolved to wait still one more day before alarming the neighbors. The next day the phenomenon recurred and she sensed it was a bad sign. The neighbors helped her force open the door that had been locked for so long, and they entered the studio. They found a huge painted canvas but were astonished to see the self-portrait of the artist irresistibly emerging from every detail of the landscapes that made up the main fabric of the picture: hills, seas, plains, mountains, animals of every species, known or unknown, a color-splashed multitude, and so on. At the foot of the painted canvas lay the artist, dead now for two days (death had undoubtedly occurred just when he had finished painting, for his brushes had all been put away and his palette was clean).

"Everyone present was shaken by the expression on his face: serene and yet troubled, amazed and peaceful. The neighbors retired in silence. They all attributed the painter's death to overwork, to which the painting bore witness: he had always claimed to want to paint the consubstantial truth of the world, and here he was, no one knew by what kind of mental aberration, unable to reproduce anything but his own face! They left the old servant woman standing there alone, in the middle of the room, helpless and silently weeping the loss of her strange master."

The fire was burning low in the great censer. The Calligrapher was dropping off to sleep, the calamus fell from his hand.

He was floating through the air and the folds of his burnoose were flapping in the sea breeze like the sails of a vessel which had long been set.

Over the azure seas, the grassy stretches swept by bitter winds, the narrow straits lit vigilantly with the Aurora Borealis, his dream carried him.

He landed in a vast library smelling of mildew. He looked through the empty bays, went around the dusty bookshelves and, in the back of the room, made out his double who was leaning on his elbows over a table: the scribe of the future who stopped writing in order to stare at him at length as if in a mirror.

At the same time the two calligraphers had parallel visions: the painted canvas came to life and, as if by super-imposition, the masked face of the drunken mystic replaced the self-portrait of the artist, desperate at not having been able to capture on canvas the universe and its mysteries.

At the same time they both had the physical sensation of immersion. Together, they traveled the ocean depths, constantly brushing past moray eels, escorted by jellyfish and tufts of purple lichen. They finally discovered in the very same instant the dim reflections of the Astrolabe, immersed in order to save the memory of the world.

The Calligrapher felt the first breath of wind and did not resist its call. He lifted off the ground, left the library and its occupant, flew over the equinoctial city, buffeted on all sides with the winds, journeyed along ocean routes, and was sucked into the center of the compass rose.

A strange feeling of well-being infused him during his assumption, in inverted time: he knew that the Work would be continued, and that well after he, Ibn Moqla,[1] was dead, someone would take up the calamus once again and continue to decipher the shade shed by a rose, the tear in the veil and the enigmatic wonders of the universe.

1. Ibn Moqla, born in Baghdad in 886 (272 Hegira); he was first tax collector, then vizier in 928. Relieved of office through the painstaking care of his enemy, the police commissioner Muhamed Ibn Yâqou, he took power again in 932 under the Caliph Al-Qâhr, only to be once again overthrown, imprisoned, and mutilated. He died on July 19, 940 (328 Hegira). Politician and great admirer of literature and science, he is most remembered for his remarkable talent as a calligrapher. It was he who established the first norms of Arabic graphics from which several generations of calligraphers were to take inspiration before a second school appeared under the calligrapher Ibn Bawwab.

As for the second calligrapher, his reproduced narrative should enlighten the reader as to his identity.

The 366th Day of Leap Year

*He had grown wiser and sadder, when he
awakened on the next day*

—Coleridge

This could be the story of a fellow who would
dream of going to Harrar.

Because it's in a region of Abyssinia, the mysterious
Kingdom of Sheba.

Because our hero loves sea horses and believes in
women's legs, but prefers, when hunger calls, those
of frogs.

Because Rimbaud reportedly met Zarathustra there.

Because not a single international congress is held there.

Because he is convinced about the accuracy of the
prophecies concerning a coming world famine.

Because Senghor wrote a collection of poems entitled
Ethiopiques.

Because our hero is for freedom of speech.

Because in French, Harrar rhymes with *y en a marre* (it's
the last straw), and *coupons les amarres* (let's cut
adrift).

Because he detests a harlot named History who only
gives herself to those most violent and most idiotic,
but who fascinates him as well.

Because he supposedly had, in great secrecy and before Jean Rostand, divined the formula for the test-tube baby.

Because the russet-colored horses no longer run along the wild banks.

Because he can do nothing for the abandoned child, the bleeding bird, the idle man cut down by the rain of bullets.

Because in Harrar, no one speaks about Godard, or punk rock, or checkups, or feedback.

Because the red-headed goddess, Sahebba, was consumed in the blaze of her hair.

Because he prefers Bach and ragas to Stockhausen and Boulez (sinful auditory conservatism!).

Because the bird-serpent Quetzalcoaltl committed suicide: its first principle having devoured its second and vice versa (try and make heads or tails out of that!).

To sum up, let's say that this fellow would dream about going to Harrar because, frankly, for him it was the only thing worth living for . . .

Great, dreamy gardens of childhood.

Silver-blue secret waters, the net traps drug up nothing but a great dead moon and here and there some grimacing kites. For a very long time I ran along the beach, following the itinerant circus and its glittering acrobats. But, hiding among the graves in the naval cemetery, I could do nothing but helplessly watch as they embarked upon a ghost ship, which slowly dissolved in the mists.

And now, with all my might, I summon to my aid the minerals, the throbbing forest, the wild animals, and the elemental forces whose dull thundering vibrates in my veins.

O, power of darkness, avenge my faded youth.

Our hero could be a very well-educated person. Then, at this particular moment in the narrative, he might well get the fine idea of thumbing through an anthology of poetry, in which he would read:

> It's only but a small hole
> In my chest
> But there blows
> A terrible wind

—Henri Michaux

This is what our hero could be like: a man haunted by going back, sublimating his childhood, refusing his present, and building the dome of his future with clay the color of the horizon.

We might find our hero walking around in the streets of his hometown. Cinematographic ellipsis. We would understand that he was waiting for someone or for something.

He would walk along the street and everything before his eyes would decompose and be recomposed countless times over. The lines would be dancing the

most fantastic of ballets, the colors would be metamor-
phosing in rhythm.

Square
White

As death. White death.
Death took me on that glaring afternoon.
I can still recall the palm trees, the east wind
(El Chergui)
That sea, so calm, glassy,
So white.

Square
White
Snowy, frosted.

The Sunnite minaret is an orthodox square.
More than perfect. It takes 33 steps to
Go around it. All tradition can be contained in
A dubious handkerchief. A handkerchief perfectly
Square. The Tower cannot be scaled.
The square Tower. Its translucent walls
Prohibit all escape.
Al Hamdou lillah! Tabaraka Allah!
Language is uncreated. Forms are
Predestined moulds. The labyrinth of your streets
Has ensnared me in its infinite meanders,
Cursed square town, architectonic dogma.

White square
Square white
Square of squares
Inveterate garrote!

Rhombus
Blue
Green
Blue and Green

Green paradise of childhood, lovely infernos!
At your center, nothing but essential blasphemy
Blue
At your center, nothing but healthy revolts
Green
Rhombus
My paradise and my torture
My bitter tasting honey-hour
My imponderable.
Blue and green make yellow.
That is why
Your laugh is jaundiced.
In the dusky light
Blue and green missed their entrance
And youth fades

Circle
Red
Brick-colored

The conch washed up by the waves
Huddles in the affectionate circle of red
Because the sun is sinking at the sea-filled
horizon.

Circle
Burnt sienna
Parenthesis

A moment's affection
I can recall my past loves
The rust of my failures.

Circle
Coffee break
Automatism of living.
Beige is gripping me
Drowning me.

Triangle
Black
O, the fervid fleece of your loins
When the tropical bird
Whistles the departure
For ecstatic heights.
Triangle
Cosine
Sine
Theorem
And the friendly mornings of the battles to be

The fire smoulders under the ash
By forced march, we will breast the heights of your
Vertex
Triangle
Black
Color of hope.

Broken lines
O, my frigates

Octogon. Exagon. Hectagon.

My many-faceted and bewildered liberty
My raving and my reason
I draw on the walls of my prison
The infinite tangles of your coupling
And the peacock in the deserted park, keeps me
company
With the variegated shimmering of its feathers.

Broken lines
Colors of the rainbow.

Our hero would walk over the marble floors of an
ancient palace fallen to ruin, and before his dreamy eyes
a ballet of numbers would form . . .

3 three 3
5 five 5
7 seven 7

Numbers, I will wash you of your cabbala in revealing your secrets.

Earth.

Nostalgia for the womb

When the winds of exile blow

Over the mirages, desert irony.

Take me back into the warmth of your womb

For I was born of your loins

And, deep sleep, take me once again into your breast.

Fire.

Fire of those at the stake and of those heaven-healed

Fire of the offering.

How I long for the fire to come!

Fire of embers.

Fire of joy.

Fire of endless clamoring

and of centrifugal forces.

Stay pure of all ashes.

And let fly your blazing arrow

Out to the azure eye

Residue of the ineffable.

Water.

Water cloudy and deep

Molecules and reflections

Water serpentine and diaphanous

Silken cloth in which Narcissus is draped

When will you stop this imposture?

Earth, water and fire

3 three 3
Mystical sign for the world

When there are no more places in which to hide
        not one recess
        not one lair
When the firm ground slips away
When it will be on earth
        up above the skies
        down under the waters
The reign of universal devastation,
I will take you into my protective bosom
And it will be the return to informal spheres
        where every color will become iridescent,
        for the sun will fecundate the moon

Take this love-charm and this magical *khamsa*[2]
For the time when finitudes come
For the time when maledictions come
And ghosts will roam along the precipices.
    Eternal return—intercession in the equity of the
circle
    Knotty desire.

5 five 5
Amatory sign for the world

---

2. This refers to a tooled piece of jewelry called "the hand of Fatima"
used for protection against the Evil Eye.

A white cock
A black ram
In the old yard
At the foot of patron mulberry

O, possessed one, bear me aloft
Upon the syncopation of your copper castanets
Off to Mandingo country
Where Soundiata holds his council
That I may hibernate
Amid the friendly caimans
Near the source
Where the mother waters are born.

One Orisha
Then another
And another
And still another
Slow fervent procession
Out to Turtle Oued!
The melted lead hardens in the swirling water.
It forms the oxidized continents of elsewhere,
The steep puzzles of the future.
7 candelabras and their waxen fingers
                              White magic
7 sacrificial swords
                              Black magic
White smoke, Black blood

                              7 seven 7
                    Magical sign for the world

To sum up, let's say that what is to be salvaged from the wreck would be as Paul Valéry suggests: . . . *a bit of free thinking, a bit of a feeling for numbers, a bit of logic, and a bit of symbolics, all of which contradict what they affirm.*

In the deserted street, the footsteps of our hero ring out . . .

Put a tiger in your tank . . .
Blue indigo. Amethyst. Lapis lazuli . . .
Buy "Têtu" stockings . . .
Vaults in broken lines. Inverted arcades . . .
Omo makes your whites whiter . . .
Citadel at the end of the world . . .
Coming soon to the city Casino . . .
The Appian Way paved and shining, sidewalk . . .
Debauchery!

This is where a very important scene would come in: our hero, throat parched, would stop by an ice-cream stand. He would ask for a cone, but just as he was to pay for it, would realize in terror that he could not get hold of his change or of anything else.

Everything would just slip between his fingers.

He could no longer hold anything in his hands.

It was at that moment, emerging from one of the cones, that he would see the horrid face of Nyarla-thotep, creeping chaos, escaped from the Lovecraft novel, who would be looking at him very calmly and with an odd smile . . .

Met yesterday an Italian viscount with a goatee, accompanied by a mysterious and exciting young woman: Justine on the arm of General Johann August Suter, as Lawrence Durrell and Blaise Cendrars looked on in reciprocal bemusement.

An interminable street, very Sunset Boulevard.

A melancholy and mysterious street.

A stop for streetcars. Not for buses, for streetcars: the author firmly insists on this, out of pure egotism. Streetcars are, he finds, charged with an explosive dose of poetry. Perhaps because they make noise when they run, as do human beings; or because their ritual frames make them look like beautifully disguised dinosaur skeletons. So, a streetcar stop!

Our hero could be standing in front of it.

The metallic sound of clanking. The streetcar is coming. Our hero is still waiting there. Waiting . . . but nothing happens. It doesn't even start raining . . .

Just at that moment, from god knows where, a faceless man would appear, all muffled up in a long black cape.

He had been running behind the streetcar.

The frugal wind would carry over to our hero, very tense and for the very first time, interested: the snatches of a few words: *will come no more.* Just then our hero would turn around and, going over to a bench, flop down on it. He wouldn't say anything, but would think all the same:

My hope has turned rotten.

This could be the story of the fellow that dreamed of going to Harrar, just as well as it could not be.

"Now we have reached the end of the cycle," said the Astrolabe. "Your eyelids are growing heavy and your limbs numb. Let me rock this next sleep of yours with a story as sweet as the circle of Eternal Return, as sweet as the promise of dawn endlessly renewed after the empire of darkness.

"Shuffle through this pack of cards, pick the Queen of Spades and the Knight of Hearts and let me tell you their story of death and resurrection . . .

Back to Samarkand

*Perhaps there exists a grave that has been
twice a grave and that laughs to see tenants
both so similar and so different. . . . Life is
like a long, sleepless night.*

—Abu ala Al-Maari

The traveler pulled up on the reins of his tired
steed. The horse snorted and docilely came to
a halt. In the setting sun, the landscape that spread
before the traveler's eyes had the clarity and the eeriness
of a dream come true.

A mischievous and benevolent jinn must have led
his horse astray, disguised the familiar paths, altered the
usual points of reference: the fertility tree upon whose
branches the women hung multicolored ribbons to
make their wombs germinate, the lonely salt marshes
over which spread the tortured shadow of a salt statue
carved by wind that the rare inhabitants of these desolate stretches took to be Lot's wife, punished for having
encouraged forbidden practices in ancient Sodom (but
what was she doing at a thousand and one days' march
from her homeland?) and the seven brass-studded
bronze gates at the top of the last hill, behind which, it
was said, the seven sleepers of Ephesus had retired to
sink once again into the oblivion of everlasting sleep.

111

Several moons had passed since the traveler had left Bassora, the city of his birth grown all too familiar and all too dull, in search of the unknown.

He had been told of a secret city inhabited by fathomless mysteries and, ever since then, an irresistible desire to discover it had tormented him.

And he had set out in the direction of Samarkand, for it had become the focal point of his tropisms and obsessed him night and day ever since an itinerant poet had mentioned it to him.

He thought back to his first encounter with the emaciated bard. It was in the main square in which gathered all the barkers, storytellers, charmers of snakes with fangs carefully removed, the players of bendirs that almost never lay mute, clairvoyant illusionists, card readers deft at dice-loading and card-marking, healers, mixers of spices and heterocilite debris, the trainers of erudite monkeys, shadow-puppet players, peddlers of illusion. . . . He had cast a distracted look over all this hubbub, still picturesque in spite of its familiarity, and had resolutely walked over to the usual spot in which a blind old man continued, despite the scant popular success of his enterprise, to exercise his trade of dove trainer.

He loved the cooing of these loyal birds and the indifference with which they seemed to obey the sweet modulations coming from their old master's lips.

That day, the audience around the "dove-tamer" (this was how the scoffing public had nicknamed the old blind man) was even less of a throng than usual. To be completely honest, his audience this time was made up of a sole spectator, dressed in rags, and looking as if he were starving to death.

Silently, he watched the poetic evolutions of the tamed fowl and then, after having thrown his coin into the empty purse, with an imperceptible gesture he invited the poor wretch to follow him. To have shared with him the pleasure of this spectacle entitled the poor creature, in his opinion, to share his meal with him.

They sat down at the table and after a while the man spoke. He recounted his journeys in the service of an adventurous Knight. He described their picaresque drifting about, their good and bad fortunes, the mundane and extraordinary things they had encountered. Then he stopped talking and began to eat again. Suddenly he looked straight ahead and very quickly began to tell his fantastic story. The flow of words was jerky and rapid, the structure of the story somewhat incoherent.

The man listening to him was, however, able to understand that a woman who inspired in his master both an inexpressible desire and an unspeakable fear had declared to the Knight (whom she was holding prisoner following who knows what kind of fantastic adventures) that she was going to set him free, but that in three years to the day at three o'clock in the afternoon at the corner of a certain street in Samarkand, no matter what he did, no matter where he tried to flee in order to defer or annul this appointment, she would find him for one last embrace.

Since then, their roving had increased. The Knight spent the time that separated him from this fatal appointment dreaming up complicated tricks most likely to take him as far away from the accursed city as possible. They traveled through desolate lands, scaled snowy peaks, trailed through silent deserts, breasted seas unknown to cartographers of the day, put between themselves and the city more meanderings than described in the stories of *The Thousand and One Nights!*

But destiny is inexorable. Three years to the day at three o'clock in the afternoon, without their knowing exactly how it happened to them, the Knight and his servant found themselves in the fated street. The Queen was calmly waiting for them, sure of herself. His master stepped forward then to meet her, without saying a word, without glancing at his servant, frozen with terror. It even seemed to him, but it was surely because his mind was troubled, that his master went forward without faltering or fear, a sweet smile on his face. It was to be the last time that he was to see the Knight alive. Every trace of his existence and even the very memory of him was lost. Ever since that day, the lonely wandering servant carefully avoided playing cards, for two of them particularly terrorized him: the Queen of Spades and the Knight of Hearts.

Yes, the tale had haunted him ever since that night when the wandering vagabond had confided in him. And the desire to see the site of that strange encounter had driven him out onto hazardous roads. And now he was nearing his goal.

The streets were deserted and in the dull hush of

silence, only the crystalline song of the thousand marble fountains that were the pride of the Asian city could be heard.

Night was drawing to an end and the traveler was quite disappointed with his tour through the city. All day long he had hoped in vain to detect some signal, no matter how innocuous, that could set apart this motley and milling crowd, these pargeted walls, these sculpted doors, this marketplace identical to the one in his native Bassora. Even those ramallun, half fortune-tellers, half calligraphers, had barely excited his curiosity. Sitting cross-legged with a small pile of sand before them, they would let their thin fingers run, upon request of worried clients, and draw tortuous labyrinths, star-shaped polygons, wobbly pentagrams—ephemeral traces of the passage of their fingers displacing the grains of sand. Then, with an inspired look, they would undertake the task of deciphering these marks and reading the future.

His day had slipped by in utter and hopeless anonymity. And he had set his sights upon signs from the night. . . . But now dawn would soon break and cast a milky and tarnished light upon his blighted hopes.

A footstep, or rather the rustling of a leaf, a hand brushing up against the rock, and he saw Her.

Her long black hair was floating in the nascent breeze. And her lavender eyes were imperious. And so, he slowly let go of his steed's bridle and went forth to meet Her. The horse whinnied and reared. The beating of its hoofs set the waning stars to twinkling.

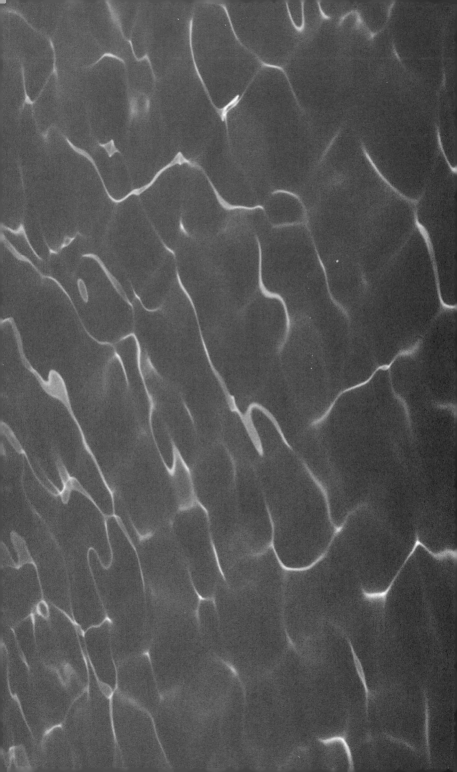